THE HENRY EXPERIMENT

Sophie Radice

© 2012 Sophie Radice

Published by Linen Press, Edinburgh 2012
1 Newton Farm Cottages
Miller Hill
Dalkeith
Midlothian
EH22 1SA

Email: lynnmichell0@googlemail.com
Website: www.linenpressbooks.co.uk
Blog: linenpressbooks.wordpress.com

ISBN: 978-0-9559618-9-2
Cover photograph: www.photoxp.co.uk
Cover design: Submarine, Edinburgh

THE HENRY EXPERIMENT

Sophie Radice

To Louis and Ella

Chapter 1

If Anna Fielding had not drunk slightly too much the night before, she would never have found Henry. It had not been a big night, only supper with their friends who lived in the next street, but the following morning, out walking her dog, Winston had raced off and she hadn't had the energy to call him back. Instead she just followed him when he turned left to run down between the ponds.

She had just straightened up from finding a good solid stick to chuck in the water when she caught sight of him – a boy wearing old-fashioned navy blue PE shorts with a faded red T-shirt under an open yellow mac. His brown hair was wet, plastered to his forehead. It was only as he took a few steps closer that she realised he wasn't wearing any shoes. His lips were moving as he muttered something to himself. She stopped and looked straight at him.

'Hello there.'

The boy carried on walking while looking down at his feet. He passed her and she turned around to follow behind him.

'Hello there. Hi. Are your mum or dad around?'

He stopped and looked up at her. He glanced at the thick stick she had in her hand. She let it drop to the ground with a thud. Perhaps it looked threatening, like a weapon. He was shivering and his lips were a pale shade of blue. His nose was running with clear snot. She bent down to talk to him.

'You're freezing. Why don't you zip your jacket up? That might make you feel a bit warmer, don't you think?'

Her instinct was to kneel down to do it for him but she thought he might not like a stranger touching him. He obliged her by doing it himself, though it took a couple of attempts for him to engage the zipper with his small cold hands. He wiped his nose on his jacket sleeve.

'So, are your parents still on the heath?'

'We went swimming in the pond. Me and my dad always go swimming in the pond.'

His voice had an American lilt. He tilted his head a little and rolled back his pale blue eyes when he spoke. There was something about the way he blinked that was a bit disconcerting. Each blink seemed to take slightly too long.

'Where is he now?'

'Oh, he went ahead of me.'

She decided to keep things light and neutral. She didn't want to suggest things to him.

'What's your name?'

'Henry.' He was shivering with cold.

'How old are you, Henry? I hope you don't mind me asking.'

He shook his head. He didn't mind.

'I'm seven, and I…'

'Yes?'

He didn't say any more.

'Well, I'm Anna and I'm forty-six, nearly forty-seven, and this is my dog Winston.'

He nodded politely. He didn't seem particularly interested in Winston. Anna had thought her dog would cheer things up and make their conversation easier.

Winston looked up. He was so used to people paying him attention and asking Anna what breed he was ('Oh, a poodle and golden retriever cross. A gold-doodle or something, I think. Ha, ha, yes, that's why he looks like a honey monster') that he seemed slightly downhearted at being ignored, particularly by a small child.

'Do you know your address, Henry?'

'Yes.'

'Could you tell me? Then I can take you there. Your mum and dad are probably wondering where you've got to, don't you think?'

He hesitated for a moment and looked up at her. Blink, blink.

'Number 23 Willowfield Road NW3 2FB.'

How odd. This was a road she knew better than any other. The road where she had been brought up and where her seventy-year-old mother still lived. Number 23 was as good as opposite. Wasn't it the Goldblatts' house? She thought it unusual that she hadn't heard from her mother that they'd moved. Usually her mother bored her with her tales of who was trying to sell up because they were getting divorced. Her mother loved stories of property and marital breakdown.

'Do you mind if I walk there with you?'

'OK. If you want.'

He set off again with his bare feet, gingerly stepping on the gravel of the main path.

'So, where are your shoes?'

'Dad hid them in a tree. He sort of does that to…'

She had to get this odd, cold little boy home right away. It was only a ten-minute walk but his parents would be frantic about him being in the park alone and with no shoes on. Perhaps he had somehow wondered off and was keeping himself calm by telling himself that his dad had gone on ahead. Kids often played at running away or taking trips. Anna remembered with a pang how her daughter Natasha had gone through a phase of getting up at the crack of dawn, getting herself dressed and packing her tiny pink rucksack, and then waiting in the shadows of the front door. Anna would come down the stairs bleary eyed to find her waiting there. She would ask Natasha what she was doing and was always told, 'I'm going on holiday to Australia.' Natasha would then sob because Anna wouldn't open the door to let her start her journey Down Under. How old was she? Three or four?

'Where do you go to school, Henry?'

'Parkside Court.'

It must be one of those private schools that were all over Hampstead, with absurd parent-pleasing uniforms complete with caps or boaters and all-year-round shorts. The mothers had the same expensive blonde highlights and collected their kids in cars like shiny, black trucks.

'Do you like school?'

'It's OK. There's another boy who knows nearly as much about dinosaurs as me. Dad doesn't want me to go back there after this term. It is too limited there. It calls itself progressive but it isn't.'

Big words for a small boy. Someone else's words.

'So what's your friend's name?'

'Faris. He's from Morocco.'

'What's your favourite dinosaur then?'

'The Yangchuanosaurus.'

'The Chinese one. Isn't it from the Jurassic period?' Anna surprised herself by pulling that out from her memory. All those dinosaur facts before bedtime had sunk in. Jason's dinosaur stage had gone on much longer than it had for other boys. It had worried her a little.

The child looked up. Blink, blink. She could tell that he was impressed that she'd known about the Yangchuanosaurus.

'The Upper Jurassic period, actually.'

'Yes. You're right, of course. Silly me.'

She'd got him interested now.

They reached the long gravel path that led to the street. She couldn't bear to see him wincing as he walked.

'Do your feet hurt?'

'Um, yes, well, they do a bit actually.'

She watched him trying to step as lightly as he could over the small, hard stones.

'Do you want a piggyback?'

His smile was beautiful and wide. It was good to see it.

'I'm not quite sure what that is. It does sound funny though. A piggyback.'

'Well, all it means is that I bend down and you get on my back and I carry you. That way we can get home a bit quicker and you won't hurt your feet so much. You want to try it?'

He looked at her as if he couldn't decide.

'Yes.'

She bent down in front of him. He lent against her.

'Put your arms round my neck. Now wrap your legs around my waist.'

It took a while until she felt that he was hanging on tight enough and that she had a good enough grip of the inside of his knees for her to stand upright with him. Her back was still strong. Perhaps giving Natasha and Jason so many piggybacks had built her back muscles. A few times she reminded him to cling tightly around her neck. When she turned her head she could smell him – muddy and pondy and snotty, and fresh and sweet as well.

She started to march up the hill with him on her back singing,

Oh, the Grand Old Duke of York,

He had ten thousand men!

She could hear him trying to sing along in her ear. She made him laugh by making him bounce up and down on her back while Winston wagged his tail.

Almost at his house, she set him down, took the lead from round her waist and called Winston to her. She asked Henry if he wanted to hold Winston's lead but he shook his head. They walked up the final stretch of the hill in silence until they came to Number 23. Her mother's house was almost opposite. Anna pointed it out to Henry.

'Look, that's where my mum lives. Number 20. The one with the red door and the purple flowers.'

The boy looked over the road and blinked one of his long blinks.

'The windows are very dirty.'

He was right. There was a film of grime over the glass of her mother's windows.

'Well, my mother drinks too much. It makes her quite messy.'

She hadn't confessed this even to her own children. She wondered why she had said it to him. He didn't respond.

The Goldblatts' house had a fashionably pale grey, shiny door. They walked up the deep steps and Anna rang the bell. The door was opened by a man who must have been at least six and a half feet tall. Anna's next thought was that he looked too old to be this child's father. Henry slipped in the door, under the man's arm, without speaking to him or turning to say goodbye to her. He almost floated in like a little ghost, Anna thought. The man carried on staring at Anna with hard, blue eyes behind round-framed glasses. He hadn't even turned to watch Henry.

'I found him on the heath with no shoes. He seemed a bit cold and lost,' Anna said, looking up at him.

The man's expression didn't change.

'He didn't have any shoes on?' Anna tried again.

The man carried on staring down at her. Unlike his son, he seemed not to blink at all. She wondered if he didn't speak English or if she had not made herself clear.

'He said you'd taken him swimming?' Anna said.

In response to her mild questions, there was an expression of contempt in his steely eyes and his letterbox mouth.

'We are very happy for Henry to find his own way home. I don't think that is beyond the remit of a seven-year-old.' His voice was American and sharp.

'Well, he didn't seem that happy. He said his feet were hurting. It's quite stony and sharp on the paths, you know.' Anna was more forthright.

'And who asked you?'

'What?' Anna heard herself say.

'Listen, lady, why don't you fuck off and mind your own business?'
He slammed the heavy door in her face.

She stepped back, her heart thumping in her chest.

'Well, fuck you too.' Her voice was quiet and shaky.

It was so far from what she'd expected. She had imagined relief or even an initial anger at the boy and she had certainly expected to be thanked for finding him and bringing him home safely. She would have replied with a small smile, perhaps raising her hand a little to deflect the praise, and said, 'Oh, it was nothing.' After all, taking a small child home was a perfectly normal thing to do. Any decent person would have done the same.

If she had not been so shocked by the tall man's reaction she would have knocked on the door again and told him it wasn't so safe on the heath, never had been, especially early in the morning or late at night. Men lived on the heath. When she was young, early in the morning on her way to school she had seen them rise up out of the undergrowth with their lumpy plastic bags. They had lurked behind trees, fiddling with themselves, and had sometimes whispered to her. Admittedly, most of them were gone now. Unspeakable Internet porn and the official, busy park wardens in too-fast vans had seen to that, but still it wasn't safe to leave a child that age to wander there alone.

Instead she just pulled Winston closer to her, stepped away from the door, thought about going to visit her mother, decided against it when she pictured her in blowsy dressing gown and chicken-feather hair, and headed back towards the car park.

Before she reached the car, the rain began with a tropical intensity. Hard, heavy, summer rain drops which soaked her in seconds through her lightweight mac. Winston jumped into the car and wiped his sodden fur over the seats, while Anna pushed her thick, wet curls away from her eyes so that she could see to drive.

Summer of Seven

The official blog of Professor Horace Henderson
BA (Yale), MS, PhD (Cornell)
June 12th 2011

The Heath:

So far I have found Hampstead Heath's worldwide reputation as a place to wander and think freely completely justified. Except perhaps on a hot day when the crowds pour in or the keep-fit groups with their screaming army instructors use it as the place to put soft-bellied professionals through their paces. Karl Marx used to picnic here, Keats was inspired here, Freud exercised here and C.S. Lewis found Narnia on a snowy day in a wood by Parliament Hill. How perfect then, that just as my son reaches the age of seven we find ourselves living not five minutes away from this magical place. There are woods and nooks and crannies you can get lost in, perfect for a small boy. Sometimes you walk out into a clearing and for a moment lose your bearings. It is in some ways more rugged and free than many places in the countryside because it has not been divided up into cultivated plots and there is no farmer shouting at you to get off his land. If you look at a map of the heath, it even looks like an Ancient Greek soldier wearing a thick leather helmet, thrusting his arm forward and leading his men into battle. The perfect place then for my boy to discover what I like to call his "warrior spirit" or his "magnificence".

Comments: 0

CHAPTER 2

David folded his large, hairy arms, forcing the silk of her red dressing gown to strain at the shoulder seams. There was an orange jewel of marmalade on his beard.

'Well, maybe it's all right for the kid to be on the heath. Did he seem lost?'

David saw things from the other person's point of view rather than from hers. Not because he was a fair person. He wasn't particularly. It was as if he needed to prove that she was wrong, and not just with him. That she was, in general, wrong.

'David, the child was seven years old and his feet were hurting. His lips were blue. You should have seen him. He was shivering.'

'Was he lost, Anna?'

She paused.

'No. He knew his way home.'

'And he knew his address?'

'Yes, he knew his address.'

David was silent for a while, as if for effect. Then he came out with it.

'You know, Anna, not everyone drives their eighteen-year-old son to football practice.'

He looked at her and raised his heavy eyebrows just a fraction.

'Look, David, I do know it's bloody odd that a kid that young is left to walk home without his shoes and I do know that it's weird for his father to be pissed off with the person who brought him back home.'

'OK, calm down. Say he is a real loon? Then you don't want to get involved anyway, do you?'

Anna stood up.

'If Henry's father is mentally ill, then surely that's all the more reason to be involved?'

She was alarmed to feel her throat constrict as if she was about to cry. She walked out and stood in the hall to calm herself. She heard him pour himself another cup of tea from the pot on the kitchen table and then the rustle of the newspaper as he resumed reading.

Anna went upstairs and phoned 999 on the barely-used landline. She wasn't sure if finding Henry could really be classified as an emergency but she didn't know what other number to ring. Her call was answered quickly and she explained to the police operator what had happened and was gratified that the man on the other end of the line took her story seriously. He immediately put her through to a female police officer who had a kind gentle voice and who asked her to tell her story again. The woman listened without interrupting.

'Well, that child is very lucky that you found him this morning and not someone else. There are some very strange people on the heath at that time of day.'

'Yes, I know. I've lived near the heath all my life. I'd never have let my kids go there on their own at that age.'

'Thank you very much and thank you for giving us his address. We'll get on to it straight away. Do you want to make a follow-up call?'

'What do you mean?'

'Do you want to ring us so we can tell you what happened?'

'Well, yes, that would be good. I didn't know that I could do that.'

The policewoman gave her a reference number and a phone number. Anna scribbled them on an old envelope and put it in her suede bag. She sat still for a moment in the chair, then with a sigh, rang her mother. She felt vaguely guilty that she had been in her street without dropping in to see her.

'Hello.'

Anna knew all the gradients of her mother's inebriation just from the first sound of her voice on the phone. This tone wasn't too bad. A few times recently she had put the phone down when her mother had answered with the slurred, syrupy speech that heralded either self-pity or aggression.

'I've got Toby and Bunch round. It's so lovely to see them.'

Toby and Bunch had seemed ancient and pickled for years. She remembered when she had taken a tiny Natasha round to see her mother and they were visiting. Toby had taken her aside and, extracting the words from his woozy head, had told her, 'If the baby ever gets too much just put her in a Moses basket and pop her on our doorstep. You know where we live don't you? We would take her in, no questions asked. OK, darling?' Anna had just about stopped herself from laughing in his face at the thought of these two drunks who could barely prop each other up being entrusted with the care of her beautiful newborn baby. 'Not if you were the last couple on earth, thank you very much,' she had wanted to say, but instead she just thanked him and told him that it was really good to know.

Perhaps Bunch's infantile name was becoming more appropriate as she reached her dotage, with Toby's beetroot red and bloated face bobbing at her side, his habitual burgundy silk cravat the only indication that he had a neck. He had reached what Anna thought of as 'The Dowager' stage of manhood earlier than most; all soft cheeks, drooping neck and turned-down mouth.

'Mum, you didn't tell me the Goldblatts had moved?'

'They haven't. They have done some sort of house swap with a famous professor. Professor Horace Henderson. Who told you that the Goldblatts weren't there, anyway?

'Oh, I can't remember now.'

'Anyway, you might have heard of him.'

'Who?'

'Professor Horace Henderson'

'No. I don't think so.'

'You know, darling, he's a well-known child psychologist or psychiatrist. I never know which. Do you? What's that?'

A voice mumbled in the background.

'Oh, Toby thinks that he's a psychologist. Anyway he's written loads of books – I think Jonathan said that one of them was called *Drowned at Birth* or something like that. They've done some sort of academic life swap with the Goldblatts. Apparently Jonathan even has the use of his second house in Ipswich, Mass, and Horace can go to their cottage in Hereford. We went there once or twice. Do you remember?'

'Have you met him?' Anna asked.

'Well, we're on nodding terms. He's terribly imminent, you know. That's what the Goldblatts said. And he's introduced me to his little boy dozens of times. Apparently people pay good money to know what he thinks about parenting.'

'You mean he's eminent. "Imminent" means that he's about to turn up at any minute. Is he?'

Anna didn't get much pleasure from correcting her mother's speech but sometimes she just couldn't help herself.

'Well, no. He's not about to turn up.'

There were sounds of background laughter. Her mother was terribly impressed by anyone well known, in any sphere. The lead singer of a heavy metal band had moved his wife and child a few doors down about two decades ago and she had boasted about them for years to anyone who would listen: 'Silver Lizard, yes. You should have seen how many cars he had. Do you know, she left the lights on all night when he was on tour? Poor woman was afraid of the dark.'

For a while a well-known chat show host had moved in with his family. Once when her mother and Anna had passed him in the street, Anna could have sworn that her mother had curtsied.

'Mum, you only curtsy to royalty.'

'What an earth are you talking about?'

'I saw you. You bent your knee.'

'Don't be silly.'

Anna found it all very pathetic.

'Is there a mother?' Anna continued.

'Yes, there is a mother. She wears those elegant Katharine Hepburn style pants. Wide-legged. They only suit a certain type.'

She didn't say 'not you' but Anna could hear it.

'Have you spoken to her?'

'As I said, you don't see her out as much. She seems younger than him. Those academics always have affairs with their students, don't they? Did I ever tell you about my affair with my tutor at art school?'

'Yes, I think so.'

Anna heard laughter in the background.

'Oh, sorry darling. Do I shock you?'

'Not particularly.'

'A funny thing… I saw the police calling there today. Bunch noticed the police car out of the window while we were eating lunch. First the poor mother opened the door and then the Professor came and a couple of police went in to the house. They came out after about half an hour. They seemed to be smiling and laughing. It can't have been anything too serious.'

Anna didn't tell her mother that she had called the police. Her mother would probably think it was perfectly normal to leave a seven-year-old to find his way home with no bloody shoes on.

Summer of Seven

The official blog of Professor Horace Henderson
BA (Yale), MS, PhD (Cornell)
June 12th 2011

My child-parenting guide "Smothered at Birth" was in the New York Times Bestseller list for at least fourteen weeks. I think that part of the reason that it so appealed to parents was that my style has always been to use many case studies (with changed names of course) to illustrate my point that children should be allowed to wander, to discover and to take risks in order to reach what I like to call "preparedness for life". This made parents able to associate and identify with the parents and children that I had seen in my professional life.

This blog is quite obviously not a guide or a paper or a clinical study but will probably be simple observations of an English summer with my son. I am new to the genre but my wife persuaded me that it would be a good way to keep my ideas flowing and communicating on my sabbatical year in the UK. In fact, I was told to use "Facebook" or "Twitter" but I found I could not condense my ideas into the necessary small blocks of words. I am already finding that it is a good daily discipline to try and get my thoughts in order and on a page of sorts and an interesting continuum of my case study approach.

Note – the English are as interfering as the Americans. More's the pity. To the woman that knocked on my door early on Sunday morning – we encourage our son to roam.

Comments: 0

CHAPTER 3

Anna opened her eyes. In the darkness of their bedroom, the sharpness of her bad dreams was already fading. She strained to recapture their vividness but couldn't remember if she had been abandoned or, even worse, had been the abandoner. Her children were stranded on a pinky-beige plastic island, one of those moulded relief maps that were piled up in her geography room at school. She hovered in the sky directly above them, looking down on their curly heads and hearing their pitiful cries... She had been so distressed with the effort of trying to lower herself and reach them that she had woken herself up.

David's snoring was unpredictable. Just when she had got used to the rhythm of it, he would move a little and the tempo would change. When he started to make a rasping noise on both the in and the out breaths, she got up and out of bed as quietly as she could. She didn't turn the hall light on but could see enough to make her way slowly down the stairs.

She let Winston into the small garden, then turned on her laptop, which waited for her on the long kitchen table stained with years of drink rings. Since Jason had started his travels, she had been looking at Facebook each day to see if he had written anything on his own page or someone else's or been tagged in a photo so that she would know that he was still alive. She was thrilled to see a little green dot by the side of his name. She quickly typed into the instant-message box and asked him to go on Skype. Right now, please! A few moments later she saw him in the strange jerky vision of the Skype screen. He seemed to be laughing at something and then was half-pixelated and frozen, locked into a huge, radiant, cubist portrait of her lovely, curly-haired boy. Then the image changed again and he was looking right at her. Did he look gaunt? Was his colour a bit yellow around his mouth?

'All right, Mum. How you doing? What time is it there?'

'Oh, I don't know, four in the morning or something. But how are you? Where are you?'

'Why you up at four? You and Dad were on the groove? No offence, but your hair looks a bit freaky.'

She saw herself in the little box in the left-hand corner of the screen. Her face was crumpled and her hair was unusually wild, even for her. She tried to smooth it down with her hand.

'I couldn't sleep. Where are you, love? I haven't been able to get though to you on the phone for a while,' Anna said.

'Yeah. My mobile's broken. I did this extreme bike ride through the mountains and I think I sat on it or something. I'm in Bolivia and...'

'What extreme bike ride?'

'In the mountains. It's called the Road of Death and an English girl died in the group just before us. She didn't turn a corner in time and just flew off the edge of the mountain by the waterfall. They don't have any emergency services here so there's nothing that can be done if you go off the side. No one helps you. I think she was alive for a couple of hours.'

Anna wanted to cry out and tell him to come home right now.

'Right. I'm glad you told me after you'd done the ride,' she laughed nervously.

'It's the risk you take if you do this stuff, Mum.' He laughed too, but his laugh was relaxed and confident.

'So, where are you?'

'Isn't it amazing that I can talk to you from some platform in the middle of the jungle, don't you think? Can you see? Just behind me...'

He ducked down and sure enough she could see bright sunshine through a mass of green, tangled leaves. A black man in a torn red T-shirt walked past the screen and Jason turned to say something to him. The man half-heartedly waved towards her.

'Who's that?'

'It's Paulo. He runs this place. I've been here for a few hours 'cause I've been talking to Ruby.'

'How is Ruby?'

Jason's girlfriend Ruby was in South East Asia. She hadn't wanted to travel with Jason but it seemed that she didn't want him to enjoy himself too much without her either.

'She's all right. We've been arguing on Skype.'

'Well, it's bound to be difficult if you are thousands of miles apart.'

'Yeah. I suppose so. It's bare hot here. I've been feeling a bit ill; shitting a bit of blood.'

'What? Are there any doctors there? Anyone you can go to?'

'Mum, I just told you. We're in the middle of the jungle. We're just about to take a boat to Colombia.'

'Is that safe?'

'Yeah. It's fine. There's one stop where we have been told to stay on the boat but apart from that it seems pretty safe.'

'Tell me about your stomach.'

'It was really hard on the bike ride because I kept wanting to crap myself.'

'Have you taken something? You've got to be careful.'

'Don't worry. I'm going to self-medicate. You know those antibiotics I was on for my throat when I left? I've got some of them left.'

'Are you sure that's wise?'

He started to say something but the screen went black. She tried phoning him through her computer again. After ten minutes and a dozen messages telling her that the caller was unknown, she gave up and lay on the sofa in the sitting room. She closed her eyes but her lids started twitching.

She had just dropped into a deep sleep when David started banging around the room. By his grim expression and the blue pouches under his eyes, she knew that her fitful night had disturbed him.

She tried smiling up at him.

'Good morning.'

He didn't respond, but kept rummaging around, looking for something.

'What're you looking for?'

'My phone. Have you seen it?'

'No. Sorry.'

'And I never have any bloody socks. You always give my socks to Jason. I'll just have to go back to washing my clothes separately.'

'Well, I'm not giving them to Jason now. Jason is in South America, so I can't really give him your socks.'

He looked at her.

'Sorry. I don't understand.'

She looked back at him. This was happening more and more. She would say something perfectly simple and he would respond as if she were speaking a strange new language. This was not a lack of communication; this was a lack of comprehension.

'Jason is in Bolivia, so that's why I said that I'm not giving him your socks at the moment.'

'What do you mean?'

'I'm not sure how I can simplify it any more.'

He looked at her with something close to dislike. 'Actually, I just went up to his room and reclaimed some of my socks from his drawer.'

She made it a private rule not to talk about domestic things. This was quite obviously a response to her mother's need to constantly discuss the daily ups and downs of the inside of her house.

'I just spoke to him. Apparently he has got such a bad stomach upset that he's passing blood. Also, he said he was entering Colombia by boat. Do you think that's OK? Aren't you only meant to cross borders by air, or something like that? Isn't that the advice we were given by the Foreign Office?'

David grunted.

'When I went to India in my gap year, my parents were lucky to get one blue airmail letter in the whole six months I was away. If I had a problem, I just dealt with it,' he said.

'So you're not worried about him crossing the border by boat?'

'No. I'm not.'

He left the room.

*

Although the top of the bus was stifling, and the blue nylon seat stuck to the back of her bare legs, she always preferred to climb the stairs and look down at the people on the streets. The hot weather had returned with a vengeance and she looked forward to feeling the cool, office air-conditioning, even though she knew that it dried out her skin and made her throat tight.

She knew she should be more careful about her job. Other friends working for magazines had found themselves made redundant. While they were now taking pottery courses or training to be couples therapists, she was carrying on with her civilised four-day week editing *Living Now*. Her governmental clients and the editorial directors of Sherbourne trusted her to edit the magazine, which was widely distributed in health centres and GP surgeries. She had a team of good freelance writers, sub-editors and art editors to call on. She thought she was a good manager, able to delegate and bring out the best in people simply by noticing the positive details of their contributions. Perhaps because she was married to David, and so used to knowing that her work was unimportant compared with his cancer research, she never pulled rank on her staff or hoarded power. She did not walk down the long office with her head in the air, like Caroline Daniel, the group editor of the luxury goods magazines, making cutting remarks to keep those who were twenty years her junior in their place.

Anna had just about managed to pick up the language of the new health policies and use it in her magazine. She knew that she was considered to be good with her governmental clients, many of whom seemed to be nervous of saying the wrong thing or being quoted in the magazine in a way that might upset their ever-changing superiors in the press office. So much of her job was to do with conveying the right tone. There was to be no hint of criticism of the cost-cutting measures that were radiating right across the country. She was expected to tuck a touch of humour in the stories about breast-feeding, five-a-day and flu-jabs. These days, the stories were all about taking charge of your own health, keeping fit, giving up smoking. She had got quite good at it. But when the office wasn't busy and there was no pressure to chase copy or to get to the printers, she felt a dull sense of disappointment that this was where her years of journalism had brought her. On those days, she wondered would she have been more high-powered and absorbed if she had been able to take herself a bit more seriously? Most of the time, though, she was glad that she had been able to skim along the surface of her work life without it taking her thoughts too far away from her children.

She brought in a coffee and blueberry muffin for her assistant editor, Johnny, sat down next to him and asked him about his weekend. He pushed back his shining sandy hair and smiled his wicked, cherub smile, and leaned in closer so his shoulder was touching hers. She liked the smell of amber from his old-fashioned aftershave, and admired his crisp shirts in pale colours. Today he was wearing the palest baby blue. He had added silver cube cufflinks.

'What did I get up to this weekend? Well, I went into this fish and chip shop and I noticed the bloke serving looking at me with his beautiful, brown eyes. It was late so he asked me behind the counter and we did it in the storage room. He smelt of chip fat, everything smelt of chip fat, but I didn't care, in fact I quite liked it.'

'How's Pelaam?'

Johnny's Albanian boyfriend lived in a flat paid for by a married older man and saw Johnny twice a week. The excuse for his absence was his Pilates class in St John's Wood.

'He started talking about how he felt so guilty about Neil again and it bored me to death, to be honest. I don't find his guilt very interesting anymore. I also don't believe that Pelaam has ever felt guilty about anyone in his whole life.'

She had met Pelaam in Soho, on Johnny's last birthday, and had found him arrogant and sullen. He both expected and courted attention with his Statue-of-David face, thick shiny black hair and gorgeous olive skin. But it wasn't his ravishing good looks that had made her uncomfortable. She hadn't liked the way he had shrugged when she asked him what he had got Johnny for his birthday.

'Johnny has many things, so many friends. I couldn't find what he would like as his present.'

'Take him out to eat somewhere. He loves trying out new restaurants, doesn't he?'

'Maybe, but he's getting a little too fat for me,' he said, and turned his beautiful Roman nose away to look at an opened packet of nuts on the bar. He picked them up and chucked a few in his mouth and didn't turn back to her. In the end she had given up and slid off her barstool. Like so many of the people she really liked, Johnny, she thought, should be more discerning about those he chose to love.

She didn't want to phone the police with Johnny next to her because he never politely ignored her calls. She didn't usually mind when he made comments about her conversations but this time she didn't want to have to explain anything. She touched him on the arm to get his attention.

'Would you mind going to the post room to see if that digital radio has arrived?'

'What?' Johnny looked at her as if she was mad.

'Could you go and get the radio for the letter-of-the-month winner please? See if it's there?'

'Can't we ask an intern to do it?'

'No. Can you? Sorry I just need to see what it's like? Make sure they've sent the right one.'

'Well, I'd rather not.'

'Come on, Johnny. Please.'

Johnny huffed towards the lift and Anna was able to dig around in her bag and unfold the envelope. She rang and quoted the crime number.

'About the boy who was found on Hampstead Heath?'

It was another policewoman, this time with a brisk, secretarial voice.

'Yes, well, I'd like to know what happened.'

'It says here that two officers went to the address you gave and the father said that he had a very bad stomach upset and had to get home quickly and so ran on ahead. The officers have written that they were satisfied with the father's explanation.'

Anna was silent for a minute as she took this in.

'Couldn't he have picked his kid up and run to his house? Or gone in the bushes?'

'Gone in the bushes?'

'Yes. Couldn't he have done his diarrhoea in the bushes?'

The policewoman was silent.

'I only know what is written in the report. The officers were satisfied by the father's explanation. I'm afraid that's all the information I have.'

'Why was he barefoot, then?' Anna asked.

'Again, I only know what has been written in the report in front of me.'

'I really don't believe that the dad had diarrhoea.'

The girl working on the Rolex magazine looked up, her carefully plucked eyebrows raised slightly. Anna smiled at her and rolled her eyes as if the person on the other end of the line had forced her to talk about diarrhoea – twice. The girl quickly looked away.

Didn't Johnny always say that if you wanted a day off work, you just had to say that you had diarrhoea because no one would ever question it? They wouldn't even ask you the cause of it like they might do if you said that you had been vomiting. There would be no, 'Oh, do you think you ate something?' with diarrhoea. He had used that excuse with her more than once and when she had reminded him, he had put his hand to his mouth and laughed into it.

'Bloody hell. I'm an idiot. I've shot myself in the foot, haven't I? The next time I want a day off I'm going to have to think of something truly unspeakable.'

'Like what?'

'Like piles. Like massive, incapacitating haemorrhoids or huge testicular boils. You wouldn't want to ask the details then.'

'Oh, you know me. I'm not squeamish. I'd ask you to show me'.

'So what happens if I think he's lying?' Anna said to the policewoman. She heard her sigh.

'Well, the visiting officers were confident that this was a one-off incident.'

'So that's it then?'

'Unless you think or have any other evidence that the child is being mistreated?'

'Well, I don't know.'

The policewomen's voice turned businesslike.

'Thank you for bringing this matter to our attention. We do appreciate it when a member of the public takes the time to report things to us.'

Anna put the phone down on her desk and googled 'Professor Horace Henderson'.

Johnny skated across the carpet to their desks. He brought her a boiled sweet from the large bowl that was always on Janet-from-Accounts' desk and popped it straight into her mouth. She saw the golden hairs on the back of his fingers as he did so. Oh, it was a glacier mint. Glacier mints reminded her of old men's pockets and tissue fluff but she didn't want to offend Johnny by spitting it out.

Summer of Seven
The official blog of Professor Horace Henderson
BA (Yale), MS, PhD (Cornell)
June 13th 2011

My father used to make us report to him in his study at Yale to test us on our Greek. My brother Uly was two and a half years younger than me yet his grasp of the ancient language was far greater than mine. He would try and whisper the answers to me but father would hear him and separate us. I was not punished but simply became the "protector", the brother whose physical attributes meant that he would be the soldier to the younger scholar. My father told us about "Germania" by Tacitus, which showed that Greek parents extensively trained their boys and girls in life-sustaining and life-enhancing skills and arts, and that the Greeks themselves held in highest regard the fathering techniques of the Spartans, the last Greek people to arrive in the Peloponnese.

I have thus incorporated my own academic learning as well as my personal experience in my child-rearing theories. Yet many of my belief systems about the free, robust child stem from my own father's great knowledge and understanding of the Ancient Greek attitude towards children. The key point is that there comes a time when mothers need to take a step backwards, away from their sons, and give them the chance to develop their independence and freedom.

Comments: 0

CHAPTER 4

Sometimes the young assistant designers used the offices to do freelance moonlighting work late at night and first thing in the morning. She always wanted to tell them that they didn't have to bother lurking so close to the photocopying machine to try and cover what they had printed out in big expensive, rolling A5 sheets on her account. She understood that times were tough and that they didn't get paid much.

Now it was Anna who was trying to snatch the reams of paper she had printed as soon as they came out of the copier, just in case one of the other editors or even her editorial director walked past. Soon she had a warm fat wedge of A4 printed papers with information about the Professor. She shoved them into her large shoulder bag. From a quick google, she had already learnt that Henderson was a Professor of Psychology and ex-director of the Duncan-Gelding Child Study Center in Boston and on sabbatical for a year in London. According to one web link he was giving a lecture in a couple of weeks at the Quaker Centre on Euston Road. He had published many articles in the American press, mostly on the paranoid parenting theme. She thought that he had coined the term 'bubble-wrap kids' because it seemed to appear in so many of his articles. She also saw that he had recently started a blog. He had written a couple of posts about Hampstead Heath, adding a few classical references. She didn't like the way he wrote. It was pompous and boastful. She didn't like anything about the man.

Even though her bag was quite heavy, when she walked along Tottenham Court Road she decided to turn into a late-night bookshop and see if she could find anything by the Professor. Before she went in, she tried to phone David, but he didn't pick up. This was the kind of research she used to do when she was a freelance journalist and had been given a writer or an academic to interview. Fast-scanning dense text to try to draw out as much as she could about someone in a short space of time. Speed reading, and yet taking in the information. She could usually glean enough from an evening's reading to appear as something of an expert on someone whose work she had not previously read. Their egos were sometimes massaged just enough by an obscure reference to their having lived in Liverpool for a year as a child, or by the title of one of their out-of-print works, or by their belief, delivered in a talk five years ago, that Winston Churchill was at the root of most of the armed conflict in the late twentieth century.

The late-night bookshop was surprising lively. It seemed that lots of people wanted to go and buy books and have a cup of coffee in the evening. It was hard to believe that bookshops were struggling, supposedly on their last legs.

She walked round the brightly lit aisles, trying not to be distracted by the latest paperbacks.

She had never stood in front of the Mind and Body shelves before and felt ashamed to be there. A tall black man with his hair in twists stood next to her and lent over to pick out a book. She had to bend down to look at the 'H' section and could see nothing by Professor Henderson.

She exhaled much louder then she meant to. The man turned to her.

'What are you looking for?'

Anna thought at first that he worked there, but when she looked properly at him and saw the slow smile creeping across his striking face, she realised that she was wrong. Her only way of coping with the surprising realisation that he was trying to engage her in conversation was to tell him what she wanted, as if he did indeed work there.

'I'm looking for anything written by someone called Professor Horace Henderson.'

'What does this author write about?' He spoke slowly, looking her in the eyes as if he was trying to say something else. He was pretending to work there too.

'Children. He writes about children.'

'How about the parenting section?'

When he said the word 'parenting' she could see the tip of his tongue against his teeth. She smiled and thanked him and went off to the back of the shop. The parenting section wasn't there. She had to walk past him again to find the parenting shelves. When he smiled at her again, she only gave him the slightest hint of one back. She didn't want to encourage him further.

She found two slim books. Both were brightly coloured. Each cover had a photo of a leaping child with the sun bursting through spread limbs. She pulled out the one called *How to Raise a Confident Child* and read the back: 'Children are increasingly becoming bound in bubble-wrap, put in front of screens and taxied to and fro by parents who are afraid – of everything. Poor mental health, lack of confidence and general anxiety are triggered in our kids by overprotective parents who are frightened of the wild joys of nature and the beauty of the unknown. Here Professor Horace Henderson reminds us that…'

She would buy this one, and the other called *Smothered at Birth*. She looked at the rows of titles in front of her and only recognised one from when her own children had been young.

She felt a presence directly behind her and realised that it was the man again. She thought she could feel his breath against her neck, hot through her hair. She turned around to show her face properly to him at close range. Perhaps he'd not realised that she was nearly forty-seven. Look at my face close up, and then you won't want me, she thought. Perhaps, because her hair was as dark and curly as ever, he had mistaken her for someone much younger.

He met her close gaze without flinching. He didn't run off screaming as if he had just seen that women in the film *She* who went in the eternal flame for the second time and turned into a wizened old hag. She wondered if beautiful male prostitutes worked in late-night bookstores, picking up bored middle-aged women. Perhaps it was one way of ensuring the survival of bookshops; to reinvent them as a genteel sex contact forum. She moved past him and walked quickly to the cash desk. She hadn't received admiration from a stranger for quite a while. She was slightly ashamed of how good it made her feel. She paid and left, and felt a little disappointed when her admirer did not follow her but went to the history section instead.

*

She walked her usual Roman route, the grimy vein of London. Starting in Trafalgar Square, down Charing Cross Road, Tottenham Court Road then past Goodge Street, Hampstead Road, Mornington Crescent, Camden Town, Chalk Farm and then sharp right home. She had to push through crowds going to the theatre and the big cinemas, past the tourists walking in infuriatingly slow, wide packs, loud with excitement as they turned into Oxford Street. Anna got stuck behind a large couple in acres of beige flannel whose flat bottoms seemed to take up the whole pavement. She gurned and grimaced with frustration until she was forced out into the traffic and narrowly missed being hit by a rickshaw. The driver turned and shouted at her in Cockney Italian. She slid past the man with the loudhailer from the Socialist Workers Party on Tottenham Court Road who always made her feel guilty because of her editorship of a governmental magazine. She finally hit the groups of nervy, thin-faced Somalian men with dead eyes on the bridge in Camden. With their dreadlocks and red, yellow and green hats, they tried unsuccessfully to pass themselves off as Jamaicans and offered her drugs.

'Sensi, Lady?'

She turned into her crescent and felt cheered by the familiar chaos of it. She walked past the pet shop, where plump kittens played in the shop window. Then straight through a gang of boys, black and white, most with killer dogs with heavy, ugly faces, hyena stripes and bobbing pink balls. One boy had two muscular, ginger Staffs, each with a studded collar branching out from the end of a single thick leather lead. It looked like a salivating, orange, two-headed monster. The tallest boy with the flattop afro asked politely after her family and had the decency to tell his friend to be quiet when he sniggered. She had known Bon since he was five years old and was in the same primary school class as Jason. She was always disarmed by his charm and politeness, perhaps because she knew that he was up to no good, standing outside the Chinese takeaway or the betting shop. She felt a confusing sense of gratitude towards Bon and his gangsta credibility because she knew that if anyone tried to rob Jason, all he had to say was, 'I'm a friend of Bon,' and he would immediately be left alone.

'Say hello to your Mum. Tell her to call me when she gets a chance. I'd like to see her,' Anna said.

There was a long queue outside the fish and chip shop: people were collecting their 'crescent dinner', as David called it. Anna caught the delicious hot fat smell and thought of the large chips in neat paper cones. She caught sight of the junkie mother who had once been pretty and plump with a shiny blonde ponytail but now had stick legs hidden by the folds of her light denim jeans. The woman walked so fast that her white trainers squeaked on the pavement. She turned quickly and, without any social niceties, asked Anna for a couple of quid. Anna gave her all the change she had in her pocket. The mother's brow furrowed at the confusion of different coins, and Anna couldn't help but stare for a moment at the strange, yellow, wax pallor of her face and the sprinkle of little red spots, like angry freckles, spread across her cheekbones.

The Irish matriarch from the travelling family on the estate went by on her shining burgundy mobility scooter, her large bare arms wobbling as she drove over the uneven, chewing gum-mottled pavement.

'I wouldn't give her money if I was you. She a thieving junkie and you know it.'

A couple of years ago, Anna had painted the house a light greeny-blue, so that it stood out from the cream facades of the rest of the small terrace. Why had she wanted to set their house apart with a candy colour that was common in seaside towns and upmarket Notting Hill terraces? It didn't work here. Something about that colour made the local taggers want to spray their names on it. Jason said that it was because it was just so minty blue and fresh and not to take it personally. Every so often Anna got out the paintbrush and tried to paint over the graffiti. Now there were uneven areas of not quite the same colour all over the lower part of the house and it looked tatty and patchwork.

She stepped in the hallway and was hit by a madly enthusiastic Winston. David was calling to her. She shouted 'Hello' but took her time setting down her bag and patting and calming Winston before she went into the sitting room. David was watching television with a takeaway curry spread out in foil tins on the small circular table.

'Where have you been?'

'I stopped at a late-night bookshop. I tried to phone you at eight-thirty-ish. I couldn't remember if it was tennis night or not.'

'We talked about having a curry tonight. Don't you remember?'

She couldn't remember anything about a curry.

'You didn't answer the phone,' David said.

Anna rummaged in her bag. There were all the papers that she was longing to read.

'I wasn't aware that there were any phone calls from you. Sorry.'

She found her mobile and saw that it was on mute.

'I've saved you some if you want it.'

It felt too hot for curry and she didn't want to sit on the sofa next to David and watch a documentary which seemed to be about Stonehenge. She edged her way out of the room and up the stairs.

First she had a long cool shower. Then she took out her stash of papers and lay on top of the bed, wrapped in a towel. The academic papers were hard going so she just flicked through them, but from his articles and essays and the parenting book his basic and much-repeated premise was easy to grasp. Henderson believed that a global anxiety about safety had led to the kind of parenting that produced controllable environments and the belief that children could not survive without the constant presence of a responsible adult. He argued that this mindset was continuously reinforced by public campaigns designed to frighten parents whose guilt-ridden relationship created an unhealthy intensification of family life. One article in a psychology magazine was entitled 'The Pernicious Role of Maternal Overprotection in Anxiety and Phobic Disorders in Adults and Children'. From what she could gather, he had drawn on the work of a Catchall and Taylor (1961) and a Gentleman (1972) to link various personality disorders to parents who tried to mollycoddle their children. A psychologist writing in *Psychology Today*, who did not agree with these views, pointed out how dated the references were and accused Henderson of ignoring recent research. He criticised Henderson for citing old psychological models which blamed everything on parenting and, in particular, mothering.

Then Anna came across an interview in a progressive American psychology magazine called *Mind Field*. Here, Henderson answered his critics: 'One does not dismiss good research just because it was written a few years ago. A study carried out by the University of Boston shows that today's ten- and eleven-year-olds are given a smaller and more clearly delineated (or defined) area in which they can play freely, are monitored much more intensely by their parents and have their play curtailed at the first signs of danger. Even without citing other academic opinion, my own observations of my patients and my own experience of life fully support my hypothesis, which is why I describe so many case studies in my papers and books. Case studies and qualitative research have been proven to be extremely reliable. I believe that some mental health problems are caused by parents, particularly mothers, who are not willing to cut the apron strings. In particular, I suggest that Dependent Personality Disorder (a pervasive and excessive need to be taken care of that results in submissive and clinging behaviour) is a direct result of parental over-protectiveness. When parents prevent the child from engaging in trial-and-error learning that develops a sense of independence and confidence, these bubble-wrapped kids become adults who cannot make their own decisions and have a fear of abandonment and feelings of helplessness.'

Anna lay back on the bed and took off her glasses. She had to admit that some of what Henderson said about allowing children to enjoy adventures made sense. She thought of Jason's inability to pack for South America without her opinion about each piece of clothing and equipment. Perhaps she had stifled his inability to make decisions.

David came into the bedroom. She tried to push the sheets of paper into her big suede bag but was too slow.

'What's all this?'

He started to take off his clothes, letting them drop to the floor. She looked, out of the corner of her eye, as she always did, at his still-slim, taut body, his high buttocks, the covering of dark hair on his chest. Her husband was a scientist with a good body. Compared to his colleagues with their soft stomachs and pale lab skin, his fine body was a rare thing indeed. His approach to his physical fitness was logical and practical. He knew that to keep everything functioning and to give himself the best chance of not getting ill, he needed to take just the right amount of exercise. No more than half an hour a day running or swimming. Nothing excessive. When he got bored with that, he went to the gym. Tennis was a pleasure. Cancer cells, he said, loved fat.

He looked down at her on the bed. She pulled the towel around her bottom.

'What you doing?'

'Just some reading.'

He lay down next to her and didn't pick up his book as she had expected him to do. He looked at her and spoke in his kind, soft voice.

'Hello, Anna.'

At first, his ingratiating approach irritated her, because he was interrupting her reading, but it was so unusual for him to give her this gentle attention that she turned to look at him.

'What were you doing in a late-night book shop, then?'

'I was looking at books.'

'At books. OK, then.'

'And guess what? A man tried to chat me up when I was bending down to look at the lower shelves.'

David smiled.

'Really? What was he like? I've heard that those late-night bookshops are just pick-up joints.'

'Handsome. Dark and handsome and African and young.'

David was intrigued and brought his naked body closer to her naked body.

'Did you like the look of him?'

'Mmm, sort of.'

She felt a little coy about his interest. It made her feel uncomfortable.

'Did you want to go off with him?'

'No. But he was quite... sexy.'

'How sexy?'

'Not as sexy as you.'

'Do you like me? Do you like what you see?'

She didn't want to speak anymore so she kissed him more deeply than she had for a while. He folded into her and just as she was starting to relax into the rhythm of him, she felt him soften. She continued pushing up to him but it was like trying to ride a bike uphill when the chain had come off. She stopped and he rolled off her.

'You OK?'

He didn't answer. Just turned away in silence.

'Come on, David, it doesn't matter'

Again he didn't respond. Anna grabbed the biggest pillow and put it over her head to block out David's silence.

Summer of Seven

The official blog of Professor Horace Henderson
BA (Yale), MS, PhD (Cornell)
June 13th 2011

Boys And Knives:

Today I went to Covent Garden to buy my son a knife in one of the outward-bound shops. Not a penknife but a sheath knife. When I was a schoolboy in the 1950s, I carried a sheath knife to school each day. As a boy, you were considered strange if you didn't. I can remember the teacher in the classroom saying: "Take out your knives, boys" (for the purpose of cutting paper, etc), and in summer we would practice throwing our knives at targets on the school playing field. It was a competition.

Comments: 3

MrBojangles said:

I agree. Learning to handle knives is an important part of growing up. I was given my first hunting gun at nine. My father taught me how to respect weaponry so that I understood the damage they could cause if they were used irresponsibly. If a young man has no knowledge of weapons then he is more likely to see it as a way of harming or terrorizing other humans rather than as a way of finding food or making things. To increase the practical view of weaponry is to decrease the emotional. That way we would have far less gun and knife crime. Good for you for pointing this out. What an excellent blog! I am enjoying reading about how you taught your young son about the robust male skills.

Meddlingkids said:

I'm presuming Prof H Henderson is an American – the land of school boy killers who mow down their teachers and classmates with easily acquired guns. Thank god in this country we have more sense. Folksy nonsense can easily tip over into survivalist lunacy.

IneedTherapy said:

Let's read what the professor has to say about teaching your child how to handle a knife without extreme opinions from the gun/knife lobby or the opposite extreme. I think it is interesting that we have a blog from an academic rather than from the men living with their mums in rooms brigade. I'm glad I stumbled upon this.

CHAPTER 5

The following Sunday Anna got up quietly, dressed quickly and slipped out into the hall. The house was full of images of her children on one sunny beach or another. There were no reminders of gloomy mornings trudging up the hill to school, or David telling them over supper to close their bloody mouths or mocking them for their lack of knowledge about something he had known at their age.

If you believed the evidence of the photos on their walls, they had spent a lifetime burying one another up to the neck in creamy sands, running over wet, wave-ridged English or Welsh beaches littered with black worm casts or pushing one other around in turquoise, sparkling Mediterranean waters. In her favourite photo, placed on the top of the neglected piano, the children were captured mid-air, jumping off a glowing honey-coloured rock that jutted out of the sea. Natasha's hair was streaming out above her; Jason was grinning like a wild boy, one hand reaching up towards the sun.

Winston pulled her out of the door and she watched his silhouette on the pavement, his shaggy outline magnified in the low morning light. The children used to say that the shadow dog was Winston 'monsterfied'. She walked fast, past the train station and then into the heath by the Lido, passing the One O'Clock club and the playground. The swings were low and the climbing frames were surrounded by a spongy dark material that Anna had been told was to stop children hurting themselves when they fell off. She thought back to the swings with frayed ropes and rickety wooden climbing frames that she had loved so much as a child. There had been a swinging boat with seats that could hold twelve of them. Two children, one at each end, would push the boat higher and higher until, with a leap, they too would be onboard, but clinging on with their hands as the boat swung through its biggest arc. It set your heart pounding. Now Anna saw an adult's carefully designed project of safe fun. *Bubble-wrapped kids.*

She went up the side of Kite Hill and looked down across the field that ran beneath it towards the running track. Apart from a few die-hard dog walkers it was almost empty. Later it would be full of sunbathers and picnickers, people who didn't usually come on the heath except when a sunny Sunday brought them in droves by train and car and bus. Anna reminded herself how fortunate she was to be able to walk here in five minutes. On she went, up the hill and then left into woods filled with dappled light, until she came out at the back of the mixed swimming pond.

It did not surprise her that they were there – the only early-morning swimmers in the pond. They were instantly recognisable. The long man was doing the front crawl through the thick, dark-green water, scattering ducks into the air and away to the fisherman's pond. Dark patches of water where the large trees around the pond cast shadows became suddenly luminous as shafts of light penetrated the murky depths.

Far behind Henderson, near the jetty, Anna could see Henry's small head bobbing up and down, treading water. Then, as if remembering why he was there, he propelled himself forward with a rudimentary and awkward doggy stroke. Anna wound Winston's lead tightly round her wrist. She did not want him breaking free and alerting them to her presence.

She moved a little closer and stood at the pond-side next to a small willow and watched them. Henry kept moving forward very slowly, never catching up with his father, whose swimming dominated the whole pond, creating a swell that joggled the orange and white floats and sent a tidal wave slapping against the thick black mud of the bank. Little Henry got himself to one of the floats and held on to it, kicking his legs behind him. He looked happy enough. Perhaps she would be proved wrong, Anna thought. The Professor would turn out to be a caring kind dad who would wrap his son in a great big fluffy towel and kiss the top of his head. Then she could go away and stop worrying.

The long, pale giant of a man in brief red swimming shorts reached the ladder at the side of the lake and swung himself up, his sopping wet hair falling in a grey rat's tail down his white back. That ponytail was repulsive. She fantasised about getting some garden shears and running up behind him and chopping it off. She could see that his torso was still muscular but his skin was starting to slacken. Although he turned to check the whereabouts of his son, he said nothing to him before disappearing into the blue wooden changing hut. Anna looked carefully at the boy, ready to run down to the pond and throw herself in the water – never mind about the father – to rescue him should he seem to be struggling. Instead, the boy turned on to his back and floated, then kicked out his legs like an upside-down frog as he pushed off in the direction of the jetty.

After five minutes, she saw Professor Henderson coming towards her down the path. He was striding purposefully. For a single second, he seemed to look in her direction, making her heart loop upwards into her mouth, but he turned off to the left and she could see his long ponytail making wet patches on the back of his pale denim shirt. He took the path where Anna had first seen Henry exactly a week before.

Summer of Seven
The official blog of Professor Horace Henderson
BA (Yale), MS, PhD (Cornell)
June 19th 2011

The Bridge:

I have always believed that a boy of seven should cross the bridge from his mother to his father and that only that way can he learn what it is to be a man. Most modern men are clearly stuck on their mother's side of the bridge. A daughter needs to take a few trips over that same bridge but a son must camp firmly on his father's side, returning to his mother only if absolutely necessary and for a temporary period.

Swimming:

These past couple of weeks I have taken Henry for an early morning swim. Like my brother Uly, he is by nature a cautious, timid, bookish boy who does not particularly wish to explore outside. As a consequence, he has poor muscle tone and limited stamina. Swimming will ease him into the fitness he will soon need. After his swim, he is left to navigate the short journey home.

Comments: 1

MrBojangles said:

This blog could do with some photos to illustrate the activities and lessons you are giving your boy. Why not upload some?

CHAPTER 6

Her interest moved back to Henry. It seemed a real effort for him to get out of the thick, green water. Her instinct was to run right round the pond and to help him as she would have done her own children, but then he managed to pull himself up the metal frame and on to the jetty. He ran on his tiptoes into the changing hut and Anna came out of her hiding place. She walked past a solitary fisherman, who didn't turn his head even when Winston tried to sniff his bag. She hung around, leaning on the low railings by the pond and looking into the water, waiting until Henry turned the corner.

All of a sudden he was walking towards her and she found herself taken aback by the physical presence of him. She had been thinking so much about him in the past week, but now he was actually there, holding a small red towel and letting it fall on the ground.

'Hello there, Henry,' Anna said.

He looked up at her and a small shy smile appeared.

'My dad says that I shouldn't speak to you.'

'Oh. All right, then.'

He didn't move but looked up at her. *Blink, blink.*

'He said that he would call the police on you for giving me a piggyback.'

'OK.'

Neither of them was sure what to do now. A magpie screeched from the top of one of the pond-side trees while Winston stood stiffly next to them. Anna looked down at Winston and thought that she had never seen him stand so rigidly before. Caught in the stillness of their silence. Henry broke it.

'He says that it would serve you right for calling the police on us.'

'Well, I'm sorry, but I only did it because I wanted to make sure you were all right.'

'Dad was very angry after that.'

He shifted on to one foot, the other resting on top of it. His skinny legs made him look like a baby stork.

'I'm sorry. I didn't mean to make him angry. I hope he wasn't angry with you?'

'He was quite angry with me, but more with you. Dad is like a T.rex when he's angry.'

'Why does he want you to walk home alone, Henry?'

Henry put on a grown-up voice.

'He says that I should be free to roam as I please.'

'Does it please you?'

'What?'

'Do you want to roam?'

'Well, it's OK sometimes if I pretend I'm a wild animal.'

'Like a lion?'

'Maybe. Or maybe like a monkey who could swing from the tree tops.'

'What about the shoes? It might help you to roam a bit better if you had shoes.'

'He says that at my age his feet were so tough that he didn't feel a thing... He says that it is good to feel the ground beneath your toes. Spartan boys never wore shoes. I suppose that animals don't have shoes either, do they?'

Spartan boys? There was something on Henderson's blog about his father and Ancient Greece, wasn't there? She went on. She was just glad that he was talking to her now.

'What about your feet, though?'

'Um, they hurt quite a lot on the stony paths. A couple of times I've cut my toes.'

They both looked down at his feet. His poor little toes looked red and slightly tender.

'What does your father say when that happens?'

'I don't know really. I think that he says that it's all part of outdoor life. He tells me to wash it and that it will heal by itself.'

'So why didn't he take you to the real country, then, if he wants you to be a country boy?'

'Oh, my mother has to work in London. She's got a great job over here and Dad studied here and says that someone very important wrote about the heath and said that it was wilder then many places in the country. That no one could divide it up and plant things on it or put animals like cows and sheep on it. Anyway, Dad is going to show me the real country soon.'

His voice was quiet, so that she had to lean forward to hear him.

'What about your mum? What does she think about all of this?'

'All of what?'

'Well, all the early-morning swimming and walking without shoes.'

'That I'll come to appreciate all that he does for me when I'm a bit older. She buys me dinosaur books and doesn't always tell Dad about them. Dad doesn't like me reading all the time. He wants me out and about in the fresh air, particularly now I'm seven.'

'Why seven?'

'I don't know. Boring.'

'What's boring?'

'Your questions are boring.'

Neither of them said anything for a minute. Then Anna spoke.

'Look, shall I give you a piggyback again? I'm not scared of the police. I don't think that they can arrest you for giving piggybacks anyway. I've never heard a policeman come up and say, "I arrest you in the name of the law for giving piggybacks," have you?'

He looked at her and she almost thought that he was going to scuttle off, and she would have let him, following at a distance to make sure that he was all right, of course. Instead he walked around behind her and just stood there, and she realised that he was waiting for her to bend down so that he could get on her back again.

Once he was safely holding on to her she got up and started to walk in the same direction as last week. He felt even lighter then the week before. She let herself inhale his smell. He suddenly spoke in a much louder voice.

'Why do they call it piggybacks? Why not donkeybacks or horseybacks? Pigs don't carry things on their backs, do they?'

'Do you know, I've never thought? You're right. I really don't know.'

She made a snorting pig sound and he laughed. She remembered from the last time she had given him a piggyback that his laugh was surprisingly loud. She started to walk off in the direction of Willowfield Road.

'Not this way. I'm meeting Dad by the swing today. He's going back home first to get us some breakfast.'

'You mean in the playground? The playground swings are right down by the train track?'

'No, it's a swing in the woods. We made it together. It's made of rope.'

'Well, you direct me then. Tell me where you think I should go. Tap me on the shoulder if you want me to turn. I'll be your special robot. Not a pig but a robot.'

She walked up the steep path in the direction of Kite Hill and was surprised to feel him resting his chin on her right shoulder. She walked up the hill and felt him tap her gently on her upper left arm when she was passing a small wood.

'You want me to turn in here?' Anna said in a monotone robot voice and turned sharply like a robot. She put her head against a tree trunk as if she had walked into it. Henry's delighted laugh filled the copse.

'No, turn a bit, silly old robot.'

'I hear you, master, and obey.'

'Keep going, robot. I'll tell you when to stop.'

She tried to call Winston in the character of the robot but it seemed as if he didn't recognise his name without her normal urgent call. She stayed as the robot but asked Henry if he could call Winston instead.

'Winston,' he called.

'You will have to shout louder. I repeat, you will have to shout louder. I repeat, you will have to shout louder. I repeat...'

'WINSTON!' he shouted this time.

'You'll have to shout even louder. Louder. Louder. Louder.'

Henry shouted so loudly that Winston came scuttling round the corner like a wild ball of tangled yellow hair and pink dripping tongue. Henry snorted and laughed with satisfaction.

'Here it is. You can put me down now. This is the tree where the swing is. Can you see it?'

They both looked up at a big tree perched over a substantial dip in the landscape. The trees formed a thick canopy, with blinding, concentrated streams of sunlight. There was a thick blue nylon rope with a flat length of wood sticking out from the end of it wrapped round a branch above them.

'Did you make that?'

'Dad and me made it. He likes making things. He made a sort of house in the woods too.'

'How on earth did you get the rope to go over that branch?'

'Dad threw it up and over.'

She looked at how incredibly sweet he was with his head looking up at such an extreme angle and his hair falling back over his nape.

'And is the swing fun?'

Henry looked up at her. He screwed up his nose.

'I always think I'm going to fall right through the air.'

'Can't you tell him that?'

'No.'

'Why not?'

'He says that when he was my age, his dad used to make him and his brother swing right across a canyon. He was really tough.'

'What? The Grand Canyon?'

'Probably. It probably was the Grand Canyon. That's the kind of thing my dad had to do. Go across massive canyons, and cross enormous deserts and live in forests and stuff.'

Henry started to move around in an agitated way. Hopping from one foot to the other.

'Do you need to go to the loo, Henry?'

'Do I need to go to what?'

'Do you need to do a pee?'

Jason used to jump from one leg to the other in an effort to ignore his full bladder. They called it his pee-dance.

'No. I think you'd better go now. Dad will be back soon and he'll be very angry if he knows that I talked to you again. He'll get you arrested, probably.'

She looked down at him, blinking.

'Maybe he doesn't need to know if he is going to get so cross. I wouldn't want you to get into trouble. I'll tell you what. I'll hide in the trees again and just make sure that he comes soon, if you don't mind.'

'He'll go stark raving bonkers if he catches you.'

'Don't worry, I'm good at hiding. See you soon?'

He looked up at her with his worried expression.

'You can come and see me next Sunday if you want. Then it's the holidays and we will be here every morning. Dad says that he is toughening me up for a really big adventure.'

'Really, what's that?'

'I don't know. He didn't tell me. I just know it's going to be really, really big.' *Blink, blink.*

'OK. See you soon, Henry. Next Sunday.'

'Bye, Anna.'

He had remembered her name. It made her beam with pleasure.

Anna put Winston back on a lead and walked down the slope and into the dip. In the thickest patch of the wood, she stood and waited once more. Soon Henderson came to his son, towering over him. He didn't touch him but stood close to him. Anna was acutely aware of her own and the dog's heavy breathing. She had to tilt her head up as far as she could to see the two figures standing above her. The father gave the boy what looked like a hunk of bread and an apple. She could hear the sound of them munching and she was glad that skinny, shivering little Henry was getting something to eat.

They both ate quickly. The man lifted the small boy up and put him on his shoulders, so that Henry was standing up with his father holding on to his skinny calves. Henry reached upwards and swiped the wooden seat, whose swinging rope was wrapped around the thick branch above them. After a few attempts, with gruff sounds of encouragement from Henderson, Henry managed a shove powerful enough to make it swing up and over. It was wrapped around the branch a few times and so Henry had to repeat this action until it fell down and the seat-log hung just a foot or so off the ground. He was gently pushed forward by his father and moved slowly to the swing. Anna could see his legs straightening out so that his knees were almost locked in an attempt to put a break on having to get close to the swing. He put the piece of wood between his legs. He stood at the edge of the hollow for a few moments and turned towards his father for reassurance. Her own children would have leapt out without a moment's hesitation. The boy jumped off the side with a mighty push from Henderson and he swung right out across the empty space. Anna looked up at Henry at the moment he reached the furthest point before the force of the swing pulled him back. His face was screwed up with fear. His eyes were wide and full of horror.

She stepped back so that she moved away from them deeper into the wooded area, dragging Winston with her.

Summer of Seven
The official blog of Professor Horace Henderson
BA (Yale), MS, PhD (Cornell)
June 19th 2011

My wife, N, was one of my most impressive students, quick to leave behind the "accepted view" and to think beyond the Judeo-Christian ideal of pampering and protecting a child so that it can no longer think for itself. She seemed to rise above her maternal instincts and listen to what I had to say about what boys need.

The incident with Franky Weinfeld has been used by my enemies. I never, ever said to Franky that he could run away, never told him that he should try and live alone in the woods. All I said was that at ten he was perfectly capable of going out into the world beyond his mother's kitchen and finding out some stuff for himself. When they found him, he was fine apart from a little dehydration and weight loss – which he benefited from if the truth be known – but he told his mother right away that he had been trying to do what Doctor Henderson had told him. Those who have been jealous of my success then took their chance.

Comments: 0

CHAPTER 7

Anna strode briskly on, walking miles around the perimeter of the heath while Winston ran eagerly beside her.

Where was the child's mother in all of this? Why wasn't she stopping Henderson? Anna would just have to turn up every Sunday to keep an eye on him and reassure him. He had smiled so brightly when she said that she would see him next week. She wanted to pick him up then and there and take him home with her. She would look after him. She would let him read as many dinosaur books as he liked and feed him porridge and buttered toast for breakfast. If he lived with her, he wouldn't have to prove anything.

She found herself near the passageway that leads from the heath into Willowfield Road. About ten houses up, she saw the giant figure of Henderson coming out of her mother's front door and closing it gently behind him. Pausing for a moment, he looked across at the Goldblatts' house before striding across the road. His legs were so long that they carried him across in a couple of steps.

What the hell was he doing at her mother's house? She opened the door with her key and called out, her mouth dry. There was no answer, so she shouted louder. Where was she? She had to be here if he had just come out of the house. Another loud shout finally produced a response from the kitchen. Anna stood on the stairs.

'Mum, why didn't you answer? I've been shouting really loudly.'

'Oh, it's you, darling. Hello. I'm not used to seeing you so early on a Sunday morning. I was listening to the radio rather intently so I didn't hear. To what do I owe this honour?'

Her mother was standing at the sink. She barely turned to look at her.

'Mum. Who was that coming out of the house?'

She tried to modulate the tone of accusation but didn't entirely succeed.

'Professor Henderson was just borrowing some heath guides. What an absolutely fascinating man.'

Her mother was speaking in a crisp, clear tone. Was Anna imagining it, or was she making an effort to sound more bland than she felt? What on earth was she hiding?

'Why was he here? What did you talk about?'

'Oh, I don't know. Many things. He's a very good listener. Rather a rare thing in a man, the ability to listen.'

'Yes.' Anna still stood on the stairs, her hands on the worn banisters.

'I was telling him how hard it was to be a single mother in the old days. He asked me quite a bit about you.' Her mother finally looked at Anna and smiled.

'Why an earth is he interested in me?'

'Oh, he's not interested in you. He's never met you, has he? He's just very good at getting me to talk about myself and of course you're part of that. It's his training, I suppose.'

'Probably.'

Her mother pulled off her yellow rubber gloves, finger by finger.

'Of course, my parents bought me this house, exactly where I wanted to live. But I had to keep the whole thing going on my own and at times it was very lonely. I don't think you realise what it's like because you've always had David, haven't you?'

As far as she could remember, her mother had not done a day's paid work in her life. Walking to the studio that she rented at the top of Hampstead Hill to spend a couple of hours painting was not exactly scraping at the coal face.

'You know, most of my friends would say, "Oh Sylvie, why don't you send Anna to boarding school? That would free you up."' She spoke in the nasal whine she always used when she was imitating her friends. It made Anna's skin crawl.

'I would reply, "Oh no, I want my Anna with me. I could never so without Anna."' She used an exaggeratedly posh voice when reporting her own words.

'Well, I wasn't going to put you through what I had been through. Anyway, I thought it would be very dull here without you. You know, I still miss you dreadfully sometimes, darling. Still, it's going to be a bit easier for you to pop by now that you've got so much more time on your hands without Jason, isn't it?'

'Well, I'm still working full time, you know, Mum.'

Anna looked at her mother and recoiled at her scragginess. Her mother wore children's clothes. Tiny, weeny, little skinny jeans. When she talked, she often went all pigeon-toed and girly. There she stood with her little shoulders hunched, her toes turned inward and her head bobbing up and down as she spoke. Anna wanted to put an end to this self-indulgence before it got worse.

'You said you had a table you wanted me to move. Did you say it was upstairs?'

'Oh, yes. It's in your old bedroom. I want it in the kitchen now, if that's all right. I've bought a nice table light for it and I think it would look rather good there, don't you?'

That small round awkward table had been moved around most of the rooms in the house. Anna was sure that it had been in the kitchen before. It never quite fitted anywhere and would end up shoved in a corner. It was made of wide planks of beautiful beech wood, unpolished but smooth and shiny with age. Anna loved the mark where a large key had somehow left its dark outline in the wood.

'Do you want any help, darling?' Her mother was almost simpering.

'No, I'm fine, thanks.'

She went up the familiar stairs, which leant slightly to the right. On the first floor was the battered elegance of her mother's upstairs living room. The pictures that she knew so well still unsettled her, as if she was once more a child on her own in a big house. There was a painting of an old woman leaning over a fire in a dark room. The artist had added pale pigment to the lid of one of the woman's eyes, which made it protrude, larger than the other. Anna had always found the picture malevolent. Why would her mother want a cyclopic hag on the wall, unless it was that the two of them were in cahoots, the old woman left there to watch Anna when her mother was gone? Her big eye focused on Anna now. She moved backwards, tripping on the edge of a worn Persian rug, and went upstairs to her old bedroom.

It had been repainted a fashionable sage green. An attractive dark-wood writing desk had replaced the pink-and-white girly dressing table that her grandparents had given her on her tenth birthday. It had been her pride and joy, the one piece of bright modern furniture in a house full of dark-brown antiques. The bed was the same, though. A single brass bed that her mother had had when she was a child. It was covered with a patchwork quilt that Anna's grandmother had made for her – all blue and white hexagons. She had loved lying in her bed, reading and running her hands along the edge of the bedspread, feeling the joins of the different fabrics where her grandmother had carefully and lovingly sewn them together. It smelt vaguely of her grandmother's perfume. She and her grandmother had the same build – a big shelf and a large bottom – but no one in the family had Anna's dark curly hair. When she was young, she wondered if her father had been a traveller from the fairground that came to the heath three times a year, and not the art teacher whom she had never met. She used to imagine that David Essex looked a bit like her father, or wonder if he was perhaps her long-lost and very sexy older brother.

Anna sat on the bed and touched the cover. It was soft and worn where she used to stroke it. She felt a huge surge of love and gratitude towards her grandmother, imagining the hours of work that had gone into the beautiful blue patchwork. Anna had once hinted that her own daughter might like her old bedcover.

'Oh, that old thing. I've no idea where it is. It must be worn out. You probably wore it out with that nervous rubbing you used to do.'

Growing up had seemed so agonisingly slow as she coped with the never-ending cloying sentimentality and sudden anger meted out by her mother. One night, in the dark corridor, she had been calling her cat when her mother had come out of her room, pulling her dressing gown hastily around her. Anna was about to call 'Flip' again when she saw her mother's face. Just for a brief moment, it was vacant and dreamy. Then her expression tightened and she drew herself back like a cobra.

'What the hell are you doing up? Go back to bed, will you?' she spat.

Anna had stared back at her without answering. Her mother leant towards her, giving off a strange animal smell, the dressing gown coming open so that Anna could see her small hard breasts and dark nipples.

'Go back to bed and stay there. You won't spoil things again for me, Missy.'

Again.

Before she picked up the table, Anna went and stood by the window and looked across the street beyond the rooftops to the heath. This view had always calmed and comforted her. As a child, it had made her feel that escape might be possible, that she could get away from her mother because there were places where her mother was not. Her eyes moved downward until she was staring into the large, perfectly polished windows of the Goldblatts' house, with glass so old and fine that you could see it dripping.

She would imagine herself in her long, white nightie, floating out of her gloomy house of uncertainties and going to that other house with Rebecca and Sara, with their dark, shiny red hair, probably practising their piano or watching *Blue Peter* or playing charades or an exciting board game. The Goldblatts' was a house of laughter and shouting, playing and pets. Jonathan Goldblatt was a master gamester. He used to play cards and Scrabble, word games and 'It'. Sometimes he would turn off all the lights while Anna and the girls would try to get downstairs without him leaping out from different rooms to catch them. Once he had jumped out so suddenly, knocking into her, that she had fallen and hurt her head. Anna never forgot how tenderly he had picked her up, while asking Rebecca to turn on the lights. His skin was warm and dark and he smelt of pipe smoke. As he bent down to look into her eyes and make sure she wasn't concussed, his stubble scrapped her cheek.

'Sorry, little one. Sorry.'

The girls had once told her, 'Our Dad really likes you, you know. Much more than all our other friends.'

She had never forgotten it.

It was while she was standing there, thinking about the Goldblatts and looking across at their house with her face close up to the window, that she saw the small figure of Henry, grinning and mirroring her from across the street.

He raised his hand slowly in a secret gesture of greeting. She raised her hand too, putting her palm flat against the windowpane. She put her forehead against the window and Henry did the same. He was copying her. She made a funky chicken movement, flapping her arms and moving her head forward in small jerks, and he did the same. She was just about to make her arm into an elephant trunk to make him really laugh when a figure appeared in the background and stood directly behind him with a hand on his shoulder. A woman with dark hair cut into a mannish bob. She looked across at Anna and gave a slight smile, raising her hand a little behind Henry's own. Anna thought that she nodded her head. As Anna returned the nod, they seemed to glide back, as if their feet had wheels, into the navy-blue darkness of the room. Anna realised that her hand was still raised. She put it down and stepped back from the window.

The table was heavier then she had imagined and while she managed to get it down each flight of stairs, she had to rest on each landing to catch her breath. Leaning over the table in such tight spaces meant its edge cut into her stomach. Dizzy with effort, she was on her way down the final flight to the kitchen when the table caught the wall and pulled off a small chunk of plaster. Her mother was standing in the kitchen looking up at her.

'Look what you've done, you clumsy clot. Oh, really!' She stamped one of her little feet.

Anna looked back at her mother, who had had a glass or two of something while Anna had been in her old bedroom. She had often been called a *clot* or an *oaf* by her mother. Now, as she stood hanging on to the table, her arms shaking with the strain of its weight, she felt like hurling it downstairs and flattening her teeny, tiny, angry little mother. Instead, she carried on down, holding the top of the table so that the solid single leg stuck out in front of her, and with as much exaggerated gentleness as she could manage, she set it down.

Her mother looked at her with a face furrowed with irritation. When Anna was a child, at this point she would usually have slipped out of the room, into the narrative of a novel or to the small black-and-white television set, where she would watch back-to-back westerns and musicals. At a very early age, she had realised that her mother's anger had to run its course and that there was nothing she could do or say to calm her. Defending herself against the accusations, however false, only made the rage last longer. Even remaining in the same room, silent and self-effacing, would drive her mother to distraction. The only course of action was to remove herself completely.

Now, she turned towards her.

'Where exactly do you want the table?'

Her mother pointed towards the French windows. Anna lifted the table one more time and struggled across the room with it.

'Is that all right?'

'So, what are you going to do about the wall?' her mother asked.

'Nothing, Mum. It's not that big a dent and it was an accident.'

She climbed back up the stairs and let herself out of the front door. Her mother called out her name, her voice pathetic and breaking, but Anna kept walking.

*

David had left a note saying that he had gone to the gym. Anna stood for a while in the hall, then found herself climbing to the top of the house and into Natasha's bedroom.

She and David would really have to do something about this room. Take a lodger; turn it into a study or a dressing room. Nat rarely visited. Anna looked at the wall where photos of Natasha, triumphant in various sports, were still displayed. What a radiant child she had been, her athleticism a lovely surprise. Her natural ability seemed to come from neither of them: David had taken up tennis late and Anna had avoided all sports at school, yet from a young age, Nat had shown a raw determination that meant that she was more than good at any sport she tried.

Anna leant into one of the photos, trying to see her daughter exactly as she had been at that moment, her smile both proud and shy, and with red patches on her cheeks from her efforts. She had won the county cup for a cross-country race. But then afterwards, when her body had started to change with the onset of adolescence, she had given up completely. She no longer felt comfortable racing around. Anna had been secretly mortified to watch her daughter's fairy-like body shape slowly morphing into her own and had been disappointed that Nat was going to look like her after all. That impressive determination had finally disappeared into Natasha's teenage obsessions: shopping trips to Oxford Street, who had said what to whom, which boy had asked which girl out. By the time Natasha was in third year, Anna realised that her brave little athlete had morphed into a plump, popular, curly-haired girl, who, like her mother, tended to play for laughs and avoided achievement because it was rather embarrassing.

Natasha had pinned up a photo of Jason as a baby. Anna looked at it – so close that her nose was almost touching it. She peered into it, trying to make it come alive. She felt tears prick at the back of her eyes. She longed to touch again the dark fluffy quiff that stuck out from his head, to feel the gorgeous plumpness of his limbs, and to smell the yeasty, damp cloud of him in the night when he sat up in his cot, his fat arms reaching out to her. She longed to recapture just one more time the childish beauty of her children, to lie next to them when she kissed them at night and patted their plump bellies. She had always said that she had been glad to have had her children when she was young, but now she felt jealous of her friends who had started so much later. She would have sold her soul just to have one hour with her children when they were still small.

When Natasha could not go to sleep on a Sunday night because she was anxious about the week ahead, she would ask her mother to sleep next to her on a mattress on the floor. Anna would always comply, even when her daughter was quite old. She had not stopped until Natasha was thirteen or fourteen. David would look in at her, sleeping on a camping mattress on the floor with her arm at an awkward angle in the air. 'Cut the umbilical cord,' he would mutter through clenched teeth.

There had been a four-year gap between them – although it wasn't for want of trying. Finally the boy had appeared, falling out of her on to the floor of the hospital room, so quickly that they were alone together for a moment. A precious silent moment. Then David and the midwife had returned from whatever they had been doing and the spell had been broken. She had loved Jason quite differently from how she had loved Natasha. There had been no instant bolt from the blue when she had looked into his tiny, waxy face; rather, love had come slowly, over the first few days, as her maternal emotions had expanded to include both of her children.

One by one, she started to peel off the photos, pulling each tiny hard pea of ancient Blu-Tack from the wall, too stony now to press into a ball. She put the pictures in neat stacks on Natasha's bedside table. It took a long time and when she had finished, the wall looked scarred. She lay down on Nat's little bed and stared up at the emptiness.

She was woken by the sound of her phone vibrating on the floor next to her.

It was Natasha. 'Are you all right, Mum? You sound weird.'

'I'm fine. Just a bit knackered, that's all.'

'Has Dad spoken to you yet about coming down?'

'No. He's been busy as usual. We've both been busy.'

'Well, Dad and I spoke and he wondered if you wanted to come and see us for your birthday. He suggested the Friday for a long weekend? Maybe take the Friday off?'

Anna immediately thought about her promise to Henry. She hesitated.

'What's wrong, Mum? Were you planning something else? Something that Dad doesn't know about?'

'Oh, no. Not really. He just hasn't said anything to me about it.'

'Well, it was only recently that we talked. We only just had the idea. Do you think you could get the time off? Is it a busy time for you? Dad didn't know. You haven't seen the cottage yet and I haven't seen you for ages, Mum.'

Anna longed to see her daughter but her unease about Henry cut through her pleasure at the thought of going away. It wasn't a busy time at work. They had just put a magazine to bed. She pulled herself together.

'What a great idea. What fun!'

'Mum, when you say, "What fun", it means that you're forcing yourself to agree to something. You did have something else planned, didn't you? Come on, admit it.'

What was she thinking? This was her daughter. Her own lovely daughter.

'No. I shall look forward to it. It's about time we saw where you lived. And met Ben properly.'

'That's what I thought. Oh, and don't worry about Jason, Mum. He's having the time of his life.'

'I know. I spoke to him on Skype. I was a bit worried about him crossing into Colombia by sea. Have you heard anything?'

'Yes, he's already on the coast in Colombia, partying and lying on the beach. So... see you for your birthday? Ring me when you're leaving so I know what sort of time to expect you.'

Summer of Seven
The official blog of Professor Horace Henderson
BA (Yale), MS, PhD (Cornell)
June 19th 2011

My father said, "All ancient Greek heroes were trying to escape from their mothers – to get as far away as they could. That is why they traveled such lengths and distances." He would then tell Uly and me that in a way we were lucky because the death of our mother meant that we didn't have to escape. We were already heroes.

My father would never have admitted it, but his preparation of Uly was not quite thorough enough. My father had relied on me being there for my brother and that is not the way these things work.

Comments: 0

Chapter 8

The following day, as she was walking down the Crescent after work, she was surprised to get a call from Moisette, Bon's mother.

'Hello, my friend. Bon said that he had seen you and that you said that you wanted to see me. So why don't you call? It is too, too long. Do you think your darling will let you out tonight?'

Moisette had what she called 'a lazy tongue'. She pronounced each word in a long, drawn-out way and sometimes the words swallowed each other up. She told Anna that it was only English that was so heavy in her mouth and that her voice in French, or her tribal tongue, was like a beautiful singing bird.

Anna had to work tomorrow, but apart from that she had nothing on. David was still at the lab. She didn't want to be in the house on her own.

'You have always said you want to come to a night from my country, and then when I ask you always say, "No, I've got to do this and that and look after my babies." Bon tells me that Jason has gone far away somewhere so you are free. Apart from your biggest baby, your David. I always say David doesn't know that he is the luckiest man alive to have such a woman as you.'

'You tell him that, Moisette. I hardly see him.'

'If he doesn't even come home to take care of you and to make love to you, then you should come out with me. Perhaps you will meet a new man?'

Anna laughed.

'There is a big dance on tonight and I want you to come with me. I want you to come this time please because I want you to meet my new lover. He is too, too handsome. His name is Philippe. What a beautiful name. It sounds like a kiss. Do you agree with this? That the name Philippe sounds like a kiss?'

'No, not really.'

'Oh, come and dance to Ndambolu with me. Have I shown you how I dance?'

'Yes. You danced at the school disco. Don't you remember? You made all the dads' eyes pop out. Where's the club?'

'It's not that far. Tottenham. My brother will drive us in his nice car and we will sit back in the seats. Please be *chez moi* at eight.'

Chez moi was a flat in the large 1930s council estate which overlooked the heath. In Anna's opinion, Moisette didn't fully appreciate its unique and beautiful location but then she was still missing her father's grand compound in the Congo.

When Anna had first seen her, Moisette had been standing in the playground in full traditional dress with Bon's youngest sister tied to her back. Then Jason and Bon became friends, and they had struck up conversations at the school gates. Moisette had told Anna about some of the horrific things that had happened to her in the Congo. 'I'm telling you that those men tried to break me,' she had confided to Anna one day. 'When I first came to London I found out that they had given me hepatitis C. Then I thought I might be broken. But they couldn't. No, they couldn't break me. My father used to call me his lioness because I am so strong. I have to make myself well and strong for my children.' She paused. 'When I wake up here in London, I am confused for a moment. I ask myself where the sun has gone.'

Moisette had the ability to make Anna weep with laughter and there were only a handful of people who could do that. She remembered how Moisette had pulled up her top right in the middle of the street to display her dangly breasts – the result of feeding three children. A male driver had swerved dramatically.

Men stared at Moisette with a hungry desire. When Anna was out walking with her, she imagined some of this sexiness spilling over on to her, making her desirable too. Moisette knew that men loved her. She said it was because she understood them. With a body as powerful and muscular as hers, she said that she was almost a man herself. As the favourite child of her father's fifteen children, she had been his honorary boy.

Anna put on a red silk dress, a little black cardigan and high heels with straps that wrapped round her ankles. She played Jason's music loudly and drank a glass of ice-cold white wine. She was doing her best to get into a party mood. She applied her make-up with care and drew a sweeping line on her upper eyelids with unusual success. Just as she was gathering up her bag, she heard David's key turn in the door. She froze at the top of the stairs. He looked up at her.

'Are we going somewhere?'

She sat down on the top step. He looked up between her legs. She crossed them.

'I'm going out with Moisette. She's taking me to a Congolese night club.'

'Oh, is she? It's a Monday night and you are going to a Congolese night club. Well, lucky you.'

'Yes. I suppose that's the sort of thing we can start doing now. Going to night clubs whenever we feel like it.'

She laughed. David didn't laugh. He put down his bag with a thump.

'Is there anything to eat?'

He started to walk towards the kitchen. She called down the stairwell.

'Well, I didn't get back from work myself that long ago.'

She walked down the stairs. She didn't want an argument before she went out. Her heels click-clacked across the wooden floor.

'Nat phoned. Nice idea going down this weekend for my birthday.

I'm looking forward to that. Thanks,' Anna said.

He opened the fridge, found a carrot and stuck it in a pot of hummus. She carried on talking to the back of his crunching head.

'It will be good to meet her boyfriend properly, won't it?' she said.

He shrugged.

'Look, do you want to come out with me?'

He turned round and gave her a withering look.

'I've had a very hard day, Anna. I've given lectures to medical students and then worked in the lab. Going to a night club with Moisette is my idea of torture.'

'I just feel I ought to go because I've refused her invitations so many times and it's getting a bit rude.'

'Well, we wouldn't want you to be rude, would we?'

She decided to leave. If she stayed in the house one more minute, he would explode into one of his red-faced rages and her evening would be ruined before it had even started.

*

She walked through the large estate until she reached Moisette's block. She pressed the intercom button, whose numbers had been worn away. She climbed the dark concrete stairs that smelt of urine and bleach and stopped in front of Moisette's red door. It was already open so she walked into the narrow hallway just as Bon's ugly dog rushed out and banged his heavy muscular frame against her legs. She stumbled and leant against the wall, calling out to Moisette while the dog sniffed her crotch and grunted through its nose.

Moisette appeared and fell over the dog. She was wearing a long, bright-yellow jersey dress that clung to her frame and fell from her body, like the folds of a Greek statue. She looked stunning – a gleaming presence against the gloomy backdrop of her flat. She smelt of jasmine. Her hair was transformed by poker-straight, mirror-shiny extensions. It was impossible to believe that she was going to be fifty in a few years.

Moisette got in first with the compliments. 'Oh, you are beautiful tonight. You are so young when I look at you.'

'Compared to you, I feel like a dried prune.'

'What?'

Moisette looked at her like she was mad and then burst out laughing.

'Hey, I've missed you these last few months. When I feel a bit down, Bon says, "Mum, why not phone Anna?" I always feel better when I have seen you. He would like me to go out with you every night, I think.'

'You should phone me if you feel like going out. I've been thinking I should go out more. I'd like to.'

Moisette took Anna's hand and pulled her into the sitting room. There were the same battered-cream faux-leather sofas and the TV screen on the textured wall that was so vast it made the elegant French news reader look like she had terrible skin. Someone had painted exotic red and blue birds along the top of the wall. On a low smoked-glass table was a big plate piled with Moisette's famous chicken wings. Her youngest daughter jumped down from the seat in front of the computer and hugged Anna tightly around her waist. Anna kissed her head.

'Look at my daughter. She is a princess. We had her photographed professionally. Go and get the photo for Anna to see.'

The girl dutifully ran into her bedroom and came back with a huge, gilt-framed photo of herself dressed in a white confirmation gown with elaborate plaits piled on her head. She was smiling a strange, beatific smile that Anna had never seen in real life.

'Of course, Madame Anna does not believe in God. Did you know that, Alice? Have I ever told you that Anna doesn't believe in God?'

Alice let go of Anna and looked up at her, confused. The television was too loud, filling up Anna's head with French words and those sharp bursts of music that signal the next news story.

'Come on, Moisette. Don't start all that again,' she said.

'Oh, don't get peed by me, Anna. I'm so happy you are here.'

For a moment she was quiet. Then, 'I wanted to ask if you would mind talking to Bon. About his behaviour.'

Alice laughed and looked up at her mother.

'You mean, "Don't get peed off by me, Anna." Mum, you have to add the "off". I've told you that before. Lots of times.'

'I don't think he would listen to me any more than he listens to you, to be honest. He might have listened to me when he was little, but not now.'

Moisette pulled Anna closer. There were dark curly hairs growing on her chest and between her breasts. The sight transfixed Anna.

'Oh, you are looking at my hairy chest. Have you never noticed that before? I suppose I have just stopped trying to look like an English woman. Alice tries to get me to take it off. She gives me creams and tweezers and shavers and all these things. She spends her own pocket money on them and leaves them on my bed. I tell her that in my country, it is a sign of beauty. Men from my country love this. They love to see a woman with some hair here. That's why I am showing it off tonight. I am proud of my hair. You are going to meet my new darling and he loves the hairs on my chest. I think an English man wouldn't like this.'

'Every man seems to fancy you, Moisette. I don't think a few hairs would make any difference either way.'

Moisette laughed loudly and nodded. She leaned over to pile a plate with chicken wings. To drink, there was something peachy and bubbly in an elaborate glass with a gold ball at the stem.

Anna started to eat. Moisette sent Alice out to get Bon from his bedroom. The ugly dog begged for the chicken wing by pressing his shoulder against Anna's leg.

'You can give him a bone.'

'Really? Don't chicken bones get stuck in a dog's throat?'

'No. I'd never heard that in Africa. Only here. In the Congo, dogs eat anything they can find. Bones are good for their teeth. That's why all the dogs in England have rotten breath and rotten teeth.'

Anna ate the meat and held the bones out for the dog. He didn't seem to have any problem crunching them up.

'I was thinking before you came that I wouldn't mind trying an English man, though I know they are different from the men from my country.'

'In what way?'

The chicken was so delicious. It had a deep, smoky taste overlaid with something citrus and fresh. She took more.

'Well, men from my country wake up hard in the morning. I've heard that white men do not.'

Anna laughed. 'Who told you that? One of your boyfriends from the Congo? All men wake up hard, unless they are ill or drunk.'

Moisette sucked her teeth. 'Really. So white men are the same? That is very difficult for me to believe. My friend from the Congo slept with a white man and this is what she said.'

'Well, how old was he? Maybe he was in his seventies or eighties. Or older?'

Moisette hit Anna hard on the leg and giggled. Bon came in the door. He was so tall that he had to bend his head to get through the door frame. His jeans, like Jason's, were hanging low, exposing half of his boxer-encased bottom.

'Oh, hello, Anna. How are you? Jason's having a banging time.'

'He hasn't phoned me much. So, he has contacted you? What did he say?'

'He just facebooked and texted me a few times. He told me this and that. About the ladies he was mixing with, mostly.'

'Look at his jeans, Anna? What is that style? Why does he show his bottom?'

'Oh, they've all been wearing jeans like that for ages, Moisette. There's nothing we can do to get them to wear their jeans higher. I tried everything. I gave Jason belts, braces… confiscated his pants…'

Neither Bon nor Moisette laughed. Moisette had put on her serious face. She asked her son to sit down in the big armchair, where the television was projected on to the wall behind his head. The bottom of the screen played out on the top of his afro.

'So how's the IT course?' Anna began.

The reply was a reluctant mumble.

'Moisette, please turn down the TV. I can't hear what Bon is saying.' Not that he was saying much. Moisette seemed to find it an odd request, but lowered the volume a couple of notches.

'Tell Anna why I am so angry with you,' she demanded.

'Cos I stayed out three nights running and I don't tell her where I am no more.'

'Anna, I phoned him many, many times and he always turned his phone off to me. I was sick worrying about it. I never slept. I started to think he is still with that gang in the Crescent. He tells me "No" but I think he still is. I need to know. You will know; you live down there. Have you seen him?'

Bon looked at her. Gave nothing away. Silently dared her to continue questioning him.

A couple of years ago, Jason and Bon had got caught smoking weed on the heath. Unfortunately, it was a teacher who had spotted them. Moisette had asked Anna to intervene then and talk to her son. She said that Anna knew more about teenagers in this country. Back home in Africa, there was no such thing as adolescence and no such thing as drugs.

'OK, Bon… you shouldn't worry your mother like that. What does it take to text her and tell her where you are? Please can you do that for her? I remember once when Jason forgot and it frightened me so much.'

Bon was looking at her, smiling, his handsome head tilted to one side. He was playing a game. Waiting to see what she would do. Anna turned to Moisette.

'What's worrying you the most?'

'I found some what he calls "weed" in his room. It makes him sleepy. It makes him unable to do his college course work. It takes over him. His eyes go dead. I want him to stop. Please ask him to stop.'

Anna looked at Bon. He was shifting in his seat.

'Do you smoke a lot?'

'No. Not compared to lots of people I know. Hardly at all.'

Anna wanted to ask him about Jason but decided not to.

'Well, Moisette is unhappy about it. She thinks that it's affecting your work.'

This was ridiculous. She was just repeating what Moisette had said. They sat in silence for a minute. Moisette waved her hand towards her son.

'OK. You can go back to your smoking den, if you won't even listen to Anna. Someone who has cared for you for such a long time. You are a lucky boy. You have people who care about you and not just people from Congo but English people too. Some of your friends have no one. No one cares in the whole world. He has a friend, a white boy, who has been living alone in his flat in J Block since he was fifteen. His mother went away to Spain to live and left him alone. Poor boy, when he got arrested I had to go to the police station to collect him.'

Bon suddenly got up. He looked down at them both.

'Well, thanks for that Anna. It was very… er… helpful.'

Moisette sucked her teeth and folded her arms.

'You see what I am saying about him, Anna?'

Anna was relieved when the buzzer went. Moisette got up to lean out of the window and waved downwards. Now her voice was full of excitement. Bon slipped out of the room.

'It's John. My brother, John. He has come to take us to the dance.'

Anna had almost forgotten about the dance. The chicken and fizzy pink drink bubbled in her stomach. Moisette shouted out instructions to Bon, said goodbye to Alice, patted the dog on his anvil head, told Anna that she had some black bits from the chicken caught in her teeth, and they went downstairs, two pairs of high heels echoing on the concrete stairs.

SOPHIE RADICE

Summer of Seven
The official blog of Professor Horace Henderson
BA (Yale), MS, PhD (Cornell)
June 20th 2011

Doorstep Woman:

She is a middle-aged mother who showed ridiculous concern about Henry walking a short distance home by himself. She noticed that Henry was barefoot, which I believe is important in the summer, to harden his soles and to add to his sense of freedom, but that worried her too. To tell Henry that I spotted her hiding among the trees the other day would be to ruin the boy's last few weeks of training. I had been building up the boy's independence and ability to tap into his own resources. Last week she interfered again. She tried to spoil things, by making Henry aware that other people might perceive this important male behavior as odd or dangerous. Today, he asked an unusual number of times to be allowed to wear his shoes. If she does try to speak to him again, it will certainly put Henry to the test. Will he confess and speak to me about it? Perhaps I will find a way to warn her off without appearing unpleasant or difficult.

Comments: 5

MrBojangles said:

In my experience women do not understand these things. You should tell her straight before she spoils your adventures with your son. Get rid of the overbearing bitch.

MaJWithersspoons said:

Is this really the official blog of Horace Henderson? I brought my kids up using your books but I have to say you sound much more eccentric in your blog. Oh, and MrBojangles, you shouldn't use language like that on a parenting site.

MrBojangles said:

I wasn't aware that this was a parenting site. I thought it was a practical fathering site. "Get rid of the interfering b***h." Better?

MajWithersspoons said:

What is it about the internet that turns people into crazies who hide behind their stupid made up names.

MrBojangles said:

Tell that to my parents. This is my real name. You have just insulted generations of Bojangles.

CHAPTER 9

Tonight was the first night that she had really taken in Tottenham. Instead of being a name on a sign on the way to the M11, it was her destination. In the car, Moisette's brother played rumba and soukous, the bass so heavy that it felt like it was changing for good the rhythm of her heartbeat. Anna had always inwardly tutted when cars passed with music so loud it made the air shake and yet here she was, sitting proudly in the back of a thudding, silver-blue Mercedes with all its windows down.

'I'm showing everyone the two beautiful ladies in my car. So I will go just as slow as I like,' he said, turning his head to smile at them. His eyes met Anna's for a moment before he turned back to the wheel.

They went past the small, low-slung shops – the nail bars, Asian grocers, crowded gentlemen's hairdressers and shops that offered cheap calls to Africa. The heat and the rush of people on the streets gave Anna the impression that she was somewhere exotic, rather than ten minutes from the Seven Sisters Road.

They parked. As they walked, Moisette linked arms with Anna and pulled her close to her side.

'Look at our yellow and red dresses. We look like egg and tomato ketchup.'

'So we do. So we do,' Anna laughed.

Down a side road was a scruffy, burgundy-canopied entrance with a small queue of people waiting outside. A large, sweating man in a too-tight suit was standing at the entrance with a golden rope looped in front of him. As each person or group stopped, he bent with a loud sigh and a straining of his trousers to unhook the rope and let them pass through. Moisette muttered something, and walked slowly, deliberately, to the back of the queue. The man's eyes followed Moisette's swaying body, then he called out to her in French and beckoned them forward to the front of the queue. A few of the waiting people tutted and sucked their teeth but no one really objected. Moisette pulled her brother beside her so that they moved as a threesome. When the bouncer pushed his hand against John's chest, Moisette turned her face to him. She raised one shoulder, pouted, then gave him a dazzling smile. He couldn't resist. Who could? With a sheepish look at the queue, he let John in too.

'Oh, let's go, darlings! We are the special, special people,' Moisette said as she descended the wide stairs. Halfway down, on the landing, a young couple were locked in a passionate embrace.

'Oh, yes. I know what my children would say,' Moisette said as they squeezed past. 'They would shout, "Get a room!"'

The kissing woman peeled herself away briefly to stare at Moisette and Anna with disapproval.

The dance hall was vast. There was a confusion of lights. A band was playing on the stage, backed by a line of dancers in bikini tops and flippy orange skirts. They moved their hips with a furious energy.

'I can do this. Look at me!' Moisette was already pulling Anna into the crowd. She started to dance, bringing her knees together and opening them out, her yellow silk dress clinging to the contours of her body. Suddenly she swooped down, pulled her dress up and pushed her legs apart and then came back up to standing, turned her back to her and made her hips rotate. John danced with them for a minute before seeing someone he knew in the crowd and moving away.

'My God, Moisette. That is totally obscene.'

Moisette shrugged to indicate that she couldn't hear.

'You look rude. Very rude.'

Moisette threw her head back and laughed.

'You try.'

Anna looked around her. What would it look like – a middle-aged white woman attempting to dance like a young African, rotating her bottom and hips in an unlikely figure of eight? Not good, she decided. Instead, she swayed gently from side to side.

A man in a crisp sky-blue shiny suit jumped on to the stage and took the microphone. Moisette stopped gyrating and clapped her hands.

'It's Kwanzee. He is so, so big in Paris. We are too, too lucky to catch him tonight!'

While she was telling Anna this, two men had joined them, slipping effortlessly into their dance space and into their rhythm.

'Oh!' Moisette squealed. With one deft movement, she had her arms round one and was kissing him hard on the mouth. She pulled him towards Anna. 'This is my darling Philippe,' she shouted in her ear.

Philippe was a tall, serious-looking man with a shaved head and glasses. He wore a pink shirt and blue military blazer with gold buttons that looked much too hot for dancing. He and Anna nodded and smiled. The other man held out his hand to Anna and she felt it rude not to give hers to him. Only when he moved closer to her did Anna recognise him... The man from the bookshop. How had he managed to find her? 'We have met before. Do you remember?' she asked, leaning towards his ear.

He shook his head.

'Forgive me. How could I possibly forget meeting you. But I have.'

'Brownstones Book Shop. Do you remember? You gave me advice about where to find a book?'

'I'm so sorry. I work there three nights a week, but I'm usually too tired to notice very much. I have a day job too. Did you find your book?'

She felt an idiot. He hadn't been trying to pick her up. He was just good at his job. He probably made all women feel singled out and special when he gave them advice about finding a particular book.

'Oh yes. I found what I was looking for. Thanks.'

He smiled. He watched her dance until his movements were complementing and flattering hers. He dipped down, moving his hands upwards as if in extravagant appreciation of her body. For a moment, she wondered if he was mocking her, but in his open face there was only kindness. He let his hand touch hers, then, rising to her level, he put both hands on her hips and guided them so that they slid not just from side to side but up and down as well. She enjoyed the firm feel of his hands. She loved the way he guided her movements.

Anna was well away when Moisette tapped her on the shoulder. In fact, she jumped. 'Drink,' Moisette was miming, as Anna looked at her in a trance. There was a bar at the side of the dance floor, where all four of them now went. Anna's dance partner introduced himself as Alphonse – a name that made Anna want to laugh. A table was cleared for them and they sat down, Alphonse very close to her on the black plastic banquette. She saw how long his thigh was compared with hers and felt its warmth against her. Moisette and Philippe were giggling and whispering together. Alphonse raised an eyebrow at them and turned towards Anna.

'Have you been to a Congolese club before?'

'No. Moisette has often asked me to come.'

'Do you like it?'

'So far. So far, I love it.'

'You dance well.'

'Oh, no. I don't think so. Seeing how Moisette dances makes me feel I should sit down and watch.'

'No, really, you dance well… considering… that you have never been here before'

He asked her questions about herself, his eyes always on her –

on her eyes, her lips, sometimes swooping down over her body, but briefly and without being creepy or making her uncomfortable. He expressed what sounded like genuine surprise that she had grown-up children. He was a health visitor working in a clinic for refugees in South London. He said that it was depressing work. The bookshop was easier.

'That's why I'm out on a Monday night, I suppose. I wasn't at all sure when Philippe asked me but then Moisette phoned and said she was bringing a friend and it seemed very rude not to come.'

'How long have you lived here?' Anna asked.

'I came over fifteen years ago. Like Moisette, I was a student who had rioted against Mobutu at medical school and they were after me. I escaped to Belgium but there were too many of Mobutu's men there so I came here. I sold many things to get here. I came with nothing.'

'How did you feel when you arrived here?'

'I miss my country. I miss the big skies.'

'Where do you live?'

'Whetstone. It's all right. I share with a couple of other guys from my country.'

'You do know that not all of the country is like London, don't you? You know that we have places with views?'

He laughed. He had perfect teeth. Teeth were very important.

'I have been to Wales. I told a friend how much I missed fishing and he took me to Wales. We did fly fishing and he made me wear big rubber boots. I enjoyed it so much. And it was beautiful. But beautiful in a different way to my country.'

'How is it different?'

For a while, Alphonse seemed lost in thought. As if he were conjuring up images.

'When I looked towards the horizon in Wales, everything was within my vision. When you stare into the distance in the Congo, you stare forever. It extends well beyond what anyone can see. You can't take it in. Too much for the eyes of an individual. That's the only way I can describe it.'

His face suddenly looked sad. He turned his head. There was no band now. A DJ was on the stage, bending his head into his decks.

'Oh. This is a good dancing song. Will you dance with me again?'

This time the dancing was gentle and, with a smile, he pulled her towards him. She found herself in his arms. His neck smelt of plain white soap. A plain square block like her grandmother sometimes used to hand-wash her clothes. She knew exactly what was happening when he lowered his head. She understood that her lips would find his. He kissed her. Her body turned to liquid. She pulled away and when she tried to speak her voice was thick with desire.

'No,' she said.

Where was Moisette? She stumbled away, Alphonse still holding her hand and trying to pull her back towards him.

'Where are you going, Anna?'

Anna knew she had to go home. She was about to go somewhere from where there might be no return.

'Don't go, Anna.'

She wanted to kiss him again. When he pulled her back towards him, she felt how hard he was against her leg. She backed away, apologising, and then ran as fast as she could out into the streets of Tottenham.

Summer of Seven
The official blog of Professor Horace Henderson
BA (Yale), MS, PhD (Cornell)
June 20th 2011

Henry shares with Ulysses a sensitive and fearful nature. I am particularly concerned, therefore, that he learns to be brave, confident, and fearless now that he is seven. Ulysses never reached manhood. I have increasingly believed that this is because of the same physical and psychological weakness. With greater training and preparation he could have overcome his natural disposition.

Comments: 0

CHAPTER 10

By ten o'clock the next morning, Anna's head was throbbing. She had taken a couple of painkillers when she woke, drunk lots of water, eaten a large bowl of porridge with some brown sugar, bought a bacon bagel from Bagel Babylon on her way into work, but she still felt delicate. Just the thought of Moisette's pink fizzy drink and the burnt chicken made her want to retch.

It had been easy to get home from Tottenham because it was a Monday night and there was a wide choice of mini-cab booths glowing in the high street. The driver did not respond to her conversation opener about the weather so she had leant back into the seat and tried not to breath in the nauseating smell of the swinging forest of tree-shaped air fresheners. When she got home she went into the bathroom and half-heartedly removed some of the dark eye make-up with face cream and loo paper. Then she tiptoed into the bedroom, threw off her red dress, climbed into bed and, without giving it much thought, climbed on top of David. Alphonse's soft kiss excited her, and excited David, until finally they rolled away from each other.

David said, 'Thanks for that. Lovely,' before he fell into a deep sleep.

A kiss was nothing. She had never kissed anyone else in all the years she had been with David. It wasn't worth confessing to him because he would only be hurt for something that was now finished. David would sneer and possibly rage at her. And he would work out the reason for her excitement when she had come back from the club. That wouldn't do much for his confidence. No, she would keep it as something delightful and harmless, something that would cheer her up in bleak moments.

The sex last night had made her feel more relaxed about David, and more hopeful that he might break off from what he was doing and find a moment to talk to her. She wanted to discuss the proposed trip to their daughter's. As she pressed the numbers for his mobile, Sandra, the accounts manager, appeared. And frowned. Anna quickly replaced her phone. Sandra was someone who laughed a lot – an odd nervous laugh that was a failed attempt to disguise her dislike of Anna and some of the others who had been at Sherbourne for years. Anna looked up at a face covered in soft blonde down and wondered how old she was. Even though she wore the kind of clothes Anna should probably be wearing – wraparound jersey dresses, sculptural long cardigans and black court heels – Anna thought she was only in her late twenties. She towered above Anna, her eyes cold, her mouth showing a lot of teeth. 'Do you have time for a meeting today? I'm very busy and have lots of account clients coming in but I could make four-fifteen?'

Anna felt she was being criticised for not being busy. Her stomach lurched. She needed more carbs to calm the washing-machine acidity of her stomach. She smiled up at Sandra. 'Yes. That's fine. It would be good to have a catch up.'

'God knows what she wants,' she said to Johnny. 'If I can get through it without her knowing how incredibly hung over I am then I will have achieved something.'

At exactly four-thirteen, Sandra reappeared. Anna saw her eyes flicker over her pictures of Jason and Natasha. Did Sandra know that Anna was old enough to be her mother?

'Shall we go into the Oak Room?'

Anna nodded. This must be more important than she had imagined. The Oak Room, though not exactly the panelled study the name suggested, was a large room where the more important meetings took place. The latest editions of the company's most favoured magazines were proudly mounted behind a wall of clear Perspex. Anna noticed that *Living Now* was not among them. They both sat down; Sandra opposite Anna at the huge table. Sandra poured herself a glass of water from a blue glass bottle, which glugged loudly when she put it down. She looked at Anna and then down at her Sherbourne notebook.

'How do you feel things have been going on the account, Anna?'

It was like the parents' evenings at school when the teacher asked the very same kind of question. This was not a good sign.

'Fine. I think the clients seem happy. The response from readers seems good. We seem to be well liked by doctors, nurses and health workers, as well as health centre users.'

'Yes, the clients do seem happy with the product. So happy, in fact, that they want to take the magazine and put it online.'

'Yes, I've talked to them about that. Seems like a good idea.'

Sandra took another sip of water. Anna heard her breathe out.

'The thing is, Anna, we really need an editor who is used to working online and here at Sherbourne, we feel that it would make sense to have an editor who works both online and in print.'

Was she saying what Anna thought she was saying? If she was, then why didn't she get on with it?

'Are you trying to say I am out of a job, Sandra?'

Sandra swallowed hard. Her voice became more businesslike.

'Due to the current financial situation, the clients are obviously not willing to stump up for two editors and we really need a different skill set for online editing.'

'What's the difference? All you need are a few meta-titles and keywords and a shorter, punchier writing style. It's not such a big deal. You could send me on a course, couldn't you?'

She heard her voice shaking. Sandra kept her eyes down.

'If you are kicking me out then I would appreciate it if you got someone more senior to do it.'

Sandra went red; she pushed back her hair, once, twice, three times in rapid succession.

'Can I remind you that I am your accounts manager?'

'Well, can I remind you that I have been here over a decade and that I think I deserve to be given the sack by someone who knows me. I'm going to sit here until you get Julia. I want to hear from Julia that you no longer want me here.'

Sandra looked like she was on the verge of tears herself. Scarlet patches had appeared all over her cleavage. She got up.

'You know full well that this is nothing to do with us but about how much the client is willing to pay.'

'Get Julia.'

Anna sat alone for ten minutes, her arms folded. The longer she waited, the more her confidence ebbed. She looked around for a tissue. Would she ever get a job again? What would David say? He barely knew what she did, anyway. Could they survive on David's salary? Not really. He was surprisingly badly paid considering he was doing the most important job known to man.

Julia swept in, Julia with her frosted bouncing hair and her crisp white shirt and black trousers. She was the Editorial Director. The favourite one in the building. She managed to be elegant and warm and welcoming all at once. Anna even considered herself to be Julia's friend. They sometimes went out for meals together and talked about their children, their husbands and the boring suits at work. She would discreetly ask Anna into her office and give her self-help books, usually about male–female relationships, but sometimes about being a success at work. Anna never read them. Today Julia's face was tight and unsmiling.

'Sandra says you're a bit upset.'

'Julia, I've been told that I haven't got a job anymore, so yes, I'm a bit upset. Does that surprise you? Sandra says you need a new superperson who can do two jobs for the price of one. I know I could do it standing on my head. I'm not the slightest bit intimidated by online stuff. By the way, have you found someone already?'

Julia looked sheepish.

'Well… actually, yes we have.'

'Can I ask who it is? Anyone I know?'

Julia looked at the floor. 'It's Johnny.'

Johnny! The little sandy-haired cuckoo! He had pretended that he didn't know what Sandra was going to say! She thought back to all the times she had slagged off the way Sherbourne was run, how she had complained how boring the job was and how they had both imitated Sandra's special laugh-for-clients. She wondered if he had used that against her by revealing what her attitude was really like to those above her.

'Sorry, Anna. You know we have to be guided by what the clients want. We have been thinking hard about other roles you could take on here at Sherbourne. I mean, there is a deputy editor's job at *Supersave* magazine. I wonder if you would consider that?'

Anna raised her eyebrows. She already knew what she was going to do. Leave now. Not serve out any notice with Johnny. Just take her tax-free redundancy money and run. She got up and walked past Julia and Sandra without looking at them.

After visiting Human Resources, where people were kind but efficient and were obviously used to handing out redundancy packages, she went back upstairs to her desk. Johnny was there. She saw his pointy Adam's apple bob up and down.

'So, how long have you known that they wanted you to do my job? I didn't know you knew anything about web editing?

'They sent me on an evening course.'

She watched him as he squirmed. She saw that one of his eyelids was flickering.

'Oh, don't worry. Best of luck, Johnny. The job is as dull as ditch water. But you know that anyway, don't you?'

Considering that she had been there more than a decade, there was surprisingly little in the two drawers of her desk. A pair of navy kitten heels, some battered trainers, photos of the children and three boxes of herbal tea that she had never been tempted to try. It all fitted into a large yellow Selfridges bag. Only Liz, who had worked as her sub-editor for over three years, came up to her. She had tears in her eyes as they hugged each other.

The graphic designer she had worked with for a couple of months had clamped on his headphones.

Anna walked out of the heavy glass doors and into Trafalgar Square. When she turned back, she gave them two fingers. It was a fuck-you seventies-Sid-Vicious-leaving-the-stage exit Then she nearly tripped over her huge yellow Selfridges bag and ruined the effect. Only the Nigerian security guard at the front desk saw her. He gave a V sign back.

'Oh, I didn't mean you,' she mouthed at him but he had turned away.

Summer of Seven
The official blog of Professor Horace Henderson
BA (Yale), MS, PhD (Cornell)
June 21st 2011

Today my son showed remarkable skill following my instructions as to how to build a small domicile. He used his knife to whittle and cut sticks, listening to my suggestions as well as using his own initiative. Ideally he would be interacting with boys of his own age outside of school, but I haven't spotted any suitable candidates who won't distract him in this crucial stage of his development. A good day.

Comments: 1

MrBojangles said:
What did you build? Can I have more details? Why do you never respond to my comments? Apart from that woman I am the only follower you have. You need to treat me with more respect.

CHAPTER 11

From the top deck of the bus, Anna got a bird's eye view of a drug deal outside Foyles, saw two Chinese women arguing outside the sex emporium and watched a punk boy trying to impress a goth girl sitting on the bridge in Camden Market. When she got off, she popped into her local newsagent to get a newspaper. Niah smiled at her as he always did and asked her how she was. Niah had started wearing a headscarf in the last year. She said that she found it liberating not having to worry about whether or not to dye her hair.

'I don't wear it at home because I don't care what my husband thinks of my grey hair. What a relief.'

Anna missed Niah's hair. It was lovely and thick, black and shiny, with hardly any grey. Anna told her that she had got the sack. Niah took a sharp intake of breath.

'Oh my gosh, Anna, that seems really disrespectful. How long you been working there? It must be at least ten years.'

'It is. This slip of a girl, probably the same age as my daughter, maybe a little older, gave me the sack.'

'Oh no. That's not right. The little Madame. You must have wanted to send her to bed without any supper.'

'Or stop her watching her favourite TV programme.'

'Or given her a damn good hiding.' Niah's head bobbed from side to side to emphasise what she was saying.

Both women laughed. Niah's laugh was surprisingly raunchy. They only stopped when a red-faced, stout man in a tight white polo neck came in and stood behind Anna. She could see his large oval nipples through the thin fabric and was repelled. Quickly she offered a pound coin and turned, but Niah caught her hand and held it for a moment.

'I mean it. It's not right. They shouldn't dump you like that. Sorry, Anna. I'm sure you were really good at your job.'

Five minutes from home, Anna suddenly worried that she had left her purse in the shop. She put her bag down on a low wall outside a house just like hers but with plastic window frames and net curtains. She rummaged in it and had just spotted her purse when two boys came out of the front door. They were maybe nine or ten. She smiled at them. They didn't smile back.

'What the fuck do you think you're doing?' one said.

'I'm sorry. What do you mean?' Anna said. Her voice sounded like the Queen compared with their Crescent accent.

'Who the fuck do you think you are putting your bag down on our wall like that?'

Anna was incredulous.

'Oh, for goodness sake. I was just checking I had my purse.'

She started to walk off but one of the boys was grabbing his bike and they were on the road beside her, one of them riding pinion style, like a little knight on its metal steed. They were glittery-eyed, out for a brawl, perhaps waiting for a scatty middle-class woman because they wanted a fight. She had walked right into their trap.

'Who the fuck do you think you are? How dare you put your bag on our wall like that?' They were cycling right alongside her.

Anna was walking fast now.

'This is just silly. I didn't do anything to your wall. I just rested my bag on it. People rest their bags on my wall all the time.'

This wasn't quite true. She had a privet hedge that was too high for anyone to rest a bag on even if they wanted to.

'How dare you rest your bag in front of our house? How dare you?' they taunted.

The last thing she wanted was for them to know where she lived but they were only ten doors away now. They were deliberately following her, their cheeks flushed with excitement. Suddenly furious, she rounded on them.

'Fuck off. Why don't you fuck off, you little bastards. Fuck off and leave me a-fucking-lone!'

She screamed so loudly that she surprised herself. Her spit went flying into the air. The genteel woman who walked her overweight Labrador down the road everyday looked across at her with horror. Then she crossed the road and planted herself in front of Anna. The dog lay on the pavement. The boys had sped off, laughing.

'What a terrible way to speak to young children!'

'You don't understand…'

'Oh, for goodness' sake. You should know better. I've a good mind to report you to the police.'

She heaved the fat dog up and walked on.

'Well, fuck you too!' Anna said, but quietly.

When she got home, she tried to phone David again. Didn't he ever look at missed calls? Losing her job must be a legitimate reason for disturbing him. She imagined him in his white coat surrounded by his research assistants, hanging on his every word. They would be breathless with admiration for the great brain of Doctor David Freedman. He must be an absolute Adonis there.

She remembered that Tuesday was the night he played tennis. She would go to the Tennis Club to tell him that she had been sacked. She walked out into the street, got into the car and turned on the engine before she realised that she didn't have the address. She had never been there. Still, she knew that it was called Holly Road Tennis Club and googled it. She quickly found the address.

Anna parked outside in the street in case it was taboo for non-members to drive into the club itself. She had to walk across a large grassy area which looked like a cricket pitch, and on towards an ugly redbrick building surrounded by outdoor tennis courts that were impressively lit. Lots of people were using them. Where was David?

Then she heard his laughter carried on the summer breeze, and followed it. She found him just as he was putting an arm around his partner to congratulate her on a particularly skilful shot. Or something. She was blonde and white-skirted. No wonder he had never asked her here. His small, dark, heavy-set, large-bosomed and distinctly unathletic wife.

Although she was standing right up against the fencing, it was a few moments before he noticed that she was there. He said something to the other players and sprinted across to where she was standing. He was smiling, the sweat on his forehead glinting in the floodlights.

'Anna! Are you OK? Has anything happened? What are you doing here?'

'We'll talk when you finish.'

He looked puzzled, then worried. Worried that she was going to embarrass him in front of his tennis chums and the Germanic blonde player with the toned brown legs.

'We're nearly finished, Anna. Jane and I are about to thrash George and Linda. Shall we go out afterwards?' He jogged off before waiting for her reply.

Still standing, trying to resist the urge to hold on to the fencing above her head, which would make her look despairing and pitiful, she watched David finish the game. Her small, fixed smile hurt her face. He and his lovely partner 'Jane' worked well together, barely needing to tell each other whose shot it was. It was easy to see that this was an established partnership. Their movements were at times balletic in their consideration for each other. They were performing a routine with variations that they knew well. Anna imagined them spot-lit as if on stage. When they won a point, David slapped an arm around the blonde women's shoulders. Anyone looking on would have assumed that David and Jane were married and that Anna was the plump singleton who served as willing audience to her sporty friends.

When the match was over, David strode around the court skimming up the balls with his tennis racket. He wasn't in a hurry to be with her. At last, they left the court and wandered over to her. By now, Anna's jaw muscles were rigid with the tension of waiting. When the sandy-haired man shook her hand, she wanted to wipe the clamminess of it on her skirt.

'So you're Anna. The woman Dave's always rushing back to instead of coming out for a drink with us. I can see why now.'

His partner, a thin woman with spiky, aubergine hair dug him in the ribs but he stumbled on.

'I've got to just say, Dave and Jane don't usually beat us. In fact it's usually the other way round. What you saw tonight was a one-off. I just need you to know that. It's very important that you know that.'

He laughed and Anna nodded and smiled as best she could. David's partner smiled at her very brightly. Too brightly? David came and put his arm round Anna's waist. This was not the kind of thing that he usually did.

'I hope you don't mind if I stay in my tennis things. It's so bloody hot,' he said.

Anna shrugged. She just wanted to get away from their flushed, smiling faces. David's hand was heavy on her hip. Their rugged jollity made her desperate to slink into the shadows or to blurt out something curt and unkind that would wipe the smiles off their faces.

'No. That's fine. Whatever you want.'

The others went on ahead while David and Anna walked slowly across the grass, lit by the strong floodlights of the tennis court.

'So what is it, Anna? You've never felt the need to come and watch me play before.'

'You're right. You've never shown any interest in me watching you.'

'No. It's good. I'm just surprised to see you. That's all.'

'Your reluctance doesn't have anything to do with your very fit tennis partner, I suppose? And I mean fit in the way Jason means it.'

David laughed.

'Jane's one of the dullest women I've ever met. She's a fantastic tennis player though. A great tennis partner. That's all.'

'Should I try and learn tennis, do you think? Would it be good if I learnt tennis?'

David laughed a little too loudly.

'Tennis isn't really your thing though, is it?'

Anna stopped in her tracks and turned to look at him.

'I didn't want to be in the house on my own because I've had some…'

'Yes,' he agreed too quickly.

'What do you mean? Yes?'

'Well, there's all this business about the boy.'

'What?'

'You've been behaving strangely ever since you bumped into that boy on the heath.'

She was surprised that he had noticed.

'Well, you took the Professor's side right away. You barely seemed interested in what I was saying. Do you remember? When I came in from the heath soaked to the skin.'

He turned to her. He was struggling to find the words. She wasn't going to help him.

'I'm a bit worried about you, Anna.'

'Why are you a bit worried?'

The light from the tennis court made him look luminously pale, his black hair too great a contrast. She still became nervous when she sensed his anger. It could still explode so violently.

'Please, think about it, Anna. Please think about how it looks. I've seen the reading material under the bed. You've got piles of papers about Henderson. Why are you reading up on him, for God's sake? You're bloody obsessed with the man. And these early-morning walks. Are you checking up on them?'

'I have met Henry again.'

'Oh, for fuck's sake!'

'Look, I found him. Me. I think there is a reason for it. If it had been you, it would have been different. You probably wouldn't have noticed.'

David paused. 'Can I ask you a question?'

'Yes, of course.'

'Do you think that Professor... what's his name?'

'Henderson.'

'Do you think that Professor Henderson hurts his child? Is he physically or sexually abusive to his child?'

Anna didn't answer immediately. They had reached a bench. Just as she made the decision to sit down, the lights from the tennis court were turned out and they were plunged into darkness, as if between scenes. Once her eyes had adjusted, she could see that the nearest illumination came from the glow of orange street lights, half a cricket pitch away, dimly visible through the large, gently swaying trees. Anna could just about make out the outline of David sitting next to her. She could smell the fresh sweat on his tennis shirt. His odour had a dark, burnt undertone.

'Is he abusive, Anna?'

David didn't need stage lights for drama. Anna could hear him rubbing his temples with the tips of his fingers – something he did when seeking a solution that eluded him. 'I don't know, David.'

'Look, Anna. Isn't it just that his parenting is the polar opposite of yours? That's it, isn't it? That's what offends you?'

He spoke carefully, as if explaining something very difficult.

'There's no need to speak slowly, David. I haven't become a moron.'

'You have to understand that not every parent feels the need to be protective every second of the bloody day.'

David's breath was coming in quick, surprising bursts. For a moment she thought he was quietly laughing. Then she realised that he was crying – for the first time in all their years together. He hadn't cried when his mother had died of bowel cancer four summers ago. She had wanted him to cry then. She had wanted him and his geneticist father to stop their emotionally controlled discussions of the disease, even though she knew it was his way of coping. Why hadn't he – just once – broken out of his scientific carapace and wept like a human being? Like a son?

Anna knew that David felt keenly the irony that his life's work had done nothing to save his mother. Yet he had never spoken about it.

'What is it, David? What on earth's the matter?'

She reached out for his face and felt his wet cheeks. His tears seemed to sting the side of her hand and she wiped them on her skirt.

'What's the matter?' She tried to keep the shock from her voice.

'When I try to think back to when the children were really young, I can't seem to remember anything. I keep trying but it's as if all the memories have been erased. Do you think that can happen?' He struggled to keep control of his voice.

Anna tried to conjure up a time when David had been there. She recalled a holiday. Cornwall. North Cornwall. That was it.

'Don't you remember that camping holiday in Cornwall? When Natasha was six and Jason was two. We bought a family-sized tent from that shop off the Kilburn High Road and we were so happy because it felt like we had a second home. The kids had their own section, although I ended up sleeping with Jason because he was scared of the dark and you slept with Natasha. You bought them nets and buckets and took them to look for crabs. Jason hurt his knee and you carried him back on your shoulders because he didn't want to bend the scab?'

'Yes. Yes, I do remember that.'

He sounded relieved. Grateful even. She could hear him smiling.

'See. You can remember the kids when they were young. You don't need to be upset.'

She pulled his face to hers and kissed his mouth. It was wet with tears.

'I'm sorry. I don't know what came over me. I'm better now. How do you remember all those details?'

She remembered all those details because at the time she always knew, unlike David, that they would eventually come to an end. The children would grow up.

'Oh, I don't know. It's probably not all memory. I look at the photo albums and the photos on the wall and some of it comes back. You know how strange I am about photo albums. You know how edgy I get if I'm not up to date with the birthdays and holidays.'

'Yes. You are strange about photo albums.' He laughed and sniffed. 'My mum never had a photo album.'

'And so we have thirty or so of the massive things.'

'They are a bit over the top.'

A pause between them. For once it was not heavy with anger.

'Jason phoned the landline this evening when I popped back.'

She felt a rush of pleasure and then disappointment that it had not been her who had spoken to him.

'Really! Is he all right? What did he say?'

'He didn't want to speak to me, of course. He was insistent that I told you that he was having a great time, that he was sleeping and eating enough, and that the blood coming from his bum had stopped.'

'Good. I was so worried about that. Did he say anything else?'

'As I said. He's not particularly interested in talking to me.'

'I do hope he rings again soon.'

'Oh, and someone else phoned for you.'

She felt him turn to her through the darkness.

'Someone called Alphonse. He left a number. Who is he? His voice sounded very fruity. And what kind of name is that? It sounds like a hairdresser.'

She responded quickly, not missing a beat.

'Oh, just a friend of Moisette's. He wants me to help him fill in a form or something. I hadn't noticed the voice.' She stopped herself letting out a little nervous laugh.

Moisette must have given him her number. She felt terrified and pleased that he had tried to contact her again.

'Anyway, I gave him your mobile.'

'Oh, fine.'

She wondered if he would call.

'You know, part of me is glad they're finally gone.'

She could feel him turning towards her.

'There! I've admitted it.'

Anna was silent.

'I know you don't feel like that at all, and I realise that since Jason went to South America all you have been thinking about is that bloody child.'

Silence. More fraught and tense.

'David. I lost my job today. I've been made redundant. That's why I came here tonight. To tell you.'

He turned to her. 'Anna! Why has it taken you so long to tell me?'

'I don't know. We started talking about the children. And Henry.'

'What happened?'

'They needed someone to do an online version of the magazine and thought Johnny might do a better job than me.'

'Really? Johnny? Your handmaiden. Bloody hell. You've taught him everything he knows, haven't you? Ungrateful little shit.' He took her hand. 'Are you very shocked?'

'I don't know how I feel. It's strange to walk out of a place where you have worked for ten years and no one says a word to you really. Perhaps I've slagged it off a bit too much to everyone over the years? I never showed any allegiance to the company.'

'You've got three months redundancy though?'

'Yes.'

'Well, that's something then.'

'Are you worried about the money?'

'I think we'll be all right. For a bit, anyway.'

'Can we go and see Natasha for my birthday, then? Now that I'm free. It was nice of you to think of that, by the way.'

He got up. 'Let's go and get a drink, shall we? Let's drink to the end of the job that bored you to death.'

Summer of Seven
The official blog of Professor Horace Henderson
BA (Yale), MS, PhD (Cornell)
June 21st 2011

Uly got tired and lay down in the long grasses by a field of corn. I lay with him and gave him some water from the bottle that was tied to my side. I looked at the sky and at the sun and told him that we would have to get going if we were going to get to the nest that father had made for us to sleep in on the other side of the ravine. Our father had taught us to tell the time by looking at the sky and it was approaching six in the evening and the whole point was to get to the nest and to spend the night there together.

Comments: 1

MrBojanles said:
Where the fuck are you going with this?

CHAPTER 12

Anna waited in the car with Winston. David came out of the house clutching a plastic bag. When Anna asked him what was in it, he seemed shy about revealing its contents.

'I just got us some snacks. Some nuts, and I made some sandwiches. Is that all right?'

His tone was defensive.

'Yes. Of course it's all right. Thanks.'

In the drive through West London to hook up with the M4, Anna could see that David was suppressing his usual need to shout obscenities at other drivers or to ask her, 'Did you see that? Did you see what that car just did? Can you believe it?' She very rarely noticed the terrible transgression the other car was supposed to have made and usually just nodded her head or tutted a bit. She glanced sideways at him. He has his belt and first button undone and he let his left hand rest on her lap while he drove. He turned it palm upwards as if asking her to take it and she did. She loved the familiar feel of the cool dry skin. She looked at his huge fingers with their covering of dark hair at the base and spatula-like fingernails. In comparison, hers looked rather small and childlike. In that moment, looking at his hands, she let herself feel comforted and convinced by his continuing love for her.

As they turned off the main road, she was immediately struck by the verdant beauty of the valley they had suddenly found themselves in. The fields were a lush, bright green when most of the countryside she had seen from the M4 was already looking a little yellow and parched. Anna marvelled at how the water running in a stream was flush with the meadow even in summer. The biscuit-coloured cattle swished their tails and lazily helped themselves to the juicy looking grass. Winston put his nose out of the window and breathed in greedily and noisily, licking the new, exciting air with his long, dripping tongue. David slowed the car down so they could take in what they were seeing and stopped on a verge laced with cow parsley and forget-me-nots.

'You expect to see a plump and pretty milkmaid walking down the road with pails over her shoulders and her skirt hitched up, don't you?' David said.

'Blimey.'

'You know what I mean, don't you? It is very eighteenth-century round here, isn't it?'

Anna read out her daughter's instructions.

'She says there's a small farm on the left and then three cottages on the right set back from the road. Hers is the end one. She said in her email that we could leave the car outside.'

'Why is this the first time we've been up?'

'Well, we've both been busy.'

'You've been so preoccupied.'

'And you've just been playing a bit of tennis and, um, trying to find a cure for cancer.'

They came to a row of pretty-looking cottages. The thick, dry, wildly twisted trunk of a wisteria snaked across all three facades. The last residue of the light-purple flowers stood out bravely amongst the brown petals. Anna would have loved to see it in May. She loved the blousy glamour of wisterias with their purple, hazy bloom. They tucked the car in the small gravelled area and walked up the steps to the raised-level front garden and down a path to the cottages.

She wondered why she felt nervous, but before she could come to any conclusion she saw her daughter emerge from the shiny, navy-blue door. Her heart leapt at the sight of her. Natasha. Sweet

Natasha. Round, plump face which was a dewier, prettier reflection of hers. High cheekbones, wide-apart deep-brown eyes and a mouth whose top lip turned up delightfully under her nose. Anna used to trace that face with her finger every evening when she said goodnight to her. Natasha walked over to her and hugged her in the middle of the path. She smelt clean and lovely, just like she had always done. Winston almost knocked her down in his enthusiasm to see her again.

Her boyfriend, Ben, lurked at the narrow front door, unsure of when to come into the family scene. Thick, long brown hair, a heavy build and a beard. Nat met him in Thailand the summer before last and Anna hadn't been given enough time to get to know him. She had only met him twice in London. She looked at him now over her daughter's shoulder and wished that her husband had the wherewithal to go over to him and at least pat him on the arm and try to set him at his ease. Instead, David waited patiently for his turn to hug Natasha and so Anna went up to Ben and kissed him on the cheek. His bushy beard felt strange. Did Natasha like the feel of it?

'What a beautiful place. How on earth did you manage to find it?'

'Well, it's part of the deal for managing the watercress farm.'

'It's lovely.'

Ben smiled at her and took her bag.

After the initial awkwardness, Natasha gave them a tour of the cottage and they admired each room, making inane comments about pieces of furniture they recognised or had given her and the view out of the window.

'You seem to have turned into quite the little home-maker,' Anna said in a clipped voice. She sounded like her mother. She didn't know where that had come from. David looked at her sideways.

'I like those curtains.' Anna knew that David was trying to cover up for her.

'Dad, those curtains come from home. They were in the sitting room for twenty years. That's why you like them.'

'Thirty years, actually,' Anna said.

'Well, they are rather nice.'

Natasha laughed indulgently and took her father's arm.

'I suppose you have your mind on higher things. How's work going, anyway?'

David beamed at the question.

'Oh, I've had a stressful time. I had to get rid of someone who's been working with me for ages.'

'Oh no, Dad. That's awful. What happened?' Natasha looked at him with real sympathy and interest.

'Well, in the end it wasn't too bad. He seemed relieved in a way. I think he understood that it was nothing personal but just the university making cuts at a particular level.'

'Poor Dad. I can imagine that you'd hate doing that.'

Anna could see that he was moved by his daughter's sensitivity and interest.

'Yes, I really did hate it. You're quite right about that.'

They all went and sat in rickety chairs in the small but pretty garden out the back and drank a bottle of local white wine, which Anna found too sweet and sickly. She realised that she was being slightly cold and disapproving. She was responding to the cottage as if it were one of the dollhouses that Nat used to make out of cardboard boxes when she was playing at being grown up, with the tiny grey and fawn felt rabbit and mouse dolls she used to love so much. She wanted to tell Natasha to stop pretending and to go and pack and they would take her home and back to her own room.

She reprimanded herself. Nat was grown up and had wisely moved away from the heart of the city chaos. She was allowed to offer her parents wine in the garden and cook her own supper, without Anna jumping up and wanting to take over. Still, she wished that there wasn't a boyfriend there. It seemed like a big effort to remember to include shy, watchful Ben in the conversation. Anna didn't want to have to find out about him when what she really wanted to know was about Nat's placement, and what the children in her class were like, and whether she thought she would stay here or be coming back to London to take up a job in a school there. All conversation had to include Ben now, and because of that there were sometimes silences that would never have happened if they had been alone with Nat.

When they went on an evening walk through the valley, Winston had to be kept on the lead because of the golden cattle. They walked to a small lake that was part of the watercress farm and Anna found herself thinking of Henry. She could hardly bear the thought of his small face searching for her when he got out of the water. For a minute she wished that she hadn't come so far away from him, but then she realised how absurd it was to put someone else's child before her own, however grown up she was. She looked at Natasha up at the front with David. He was making her laugh so much that a few times she had to stop to catch her breath and lean on a tree or a fence. Anna remembered that she had always laughed in this particular way with him, cracking up, holding on to things when she was suddenly overwhelmed at something he had said. Anna never quite caught what was so funny. David didn't seem like a particularly funny man to her.

She was stuck with Ben and found it a real effort to keep the conversation going. He was good looking, with a full mouth and large, kind brown eyes. She could see from the side and when he stepped a little ahead that his T-shirt fell sculpturally on his unself-consciously muscular, burly torso. She was careful not to let her eyes rest upon him too much when he gave her his short and perfectly adequate answers. Ben seemed to be slightly uncomfortable with the way Natasha was laughing so loudly too, filling up the whole countryside with her hearty peals. He kept looking towards her with a slightly puzzled expression. Perhaps she had never laughed like that with him either. Natasha turned backwards towards them, and made her expression more sober, suddenly seeming to notice them.

'There's so much to do round here, Mum. We'll make a plan.'

'Lovely.'

'Great, Mum.'

She found herself going up to her daughter and reaching up and sweeping her hand over her chaotic curls as they stood in the meadow next to her cottage.

*

On Anna's birthday they decided to go swimming at Durdle Dor. Natasha brought them breakfast in bed, with pancakes and strawberries and cream. Birthday breakfast in bed was always a tradition with their family and Anna was glad that Natasha hadn't forgotten it. Natasha gave her a pair of long, dangly turquoise earrings and Anna managed to swallow the thought that she had never worn dangly earrings and wasn't about to. They were the kind of seventies-type earrings her own mother would wear if she was dressing up for a 'do'. Perhaps that was why Anna had always preferred neat little studs.

Parking at the caravan site at the top of Durdle Dor, they divided the picnic between them and made the long walk down towards the beach. Ben and Natasha walked on ahead and Anna noticed their easy way with each other. The night before as she and David had lain in their comfortable sofa bed in the sitting room, they had heard them. Not the sound of sex, thankfully, but a contented burble.

'They seem to get on very well, don't they, David?' Anna whispered. David didn't answer.

'They seem to get on very well, I said.'

'I don't know, Anna.'

'What's wrong? Don't you like Ben?'

David was lying on his back. Anna put her hand on his chest. She felt from the movement of his ribs that he had let out a big sigh.

'Since when has she been a bloody vegetarian? All that brown food is like being a student in Brighton again.'

'Oh, David. She stopped eating meat when she was eighteen. Come on. Don't tell me you can't remember?'

'I can't keep up with her.'

Then Anna found herself feeling quite hysterical with laughter, knowing that her daughter and her boyfriend were lying in the bed in the room directly upstairs and that it had taken David nearly five years to notice that Nat didn't eat meat.

The beach to the left of the Dor was packed, so they had climbed down the steep steps cut into the rock and through the shingles to get away from the crowds. Once they had reached a less crowded spot, Ben stretched out his already brown torso, while David found a small cave to sit half in and read a book, with a hat and a towel over his shoulders. Natasha called out to him, 'Dad, you look like a grumpy bear.'

If Anna had said that to him he would have scowled and sulked but he smiled sheepishly at Nat.

After nearly an hour of lying in the sun, Natasha and Anna looked at each other and nodded and started to run as fast as they could with the hot stones burning their feet. They crashed into the waves and Anna couldn't help shouting out as she hit the delicious cold of the water. They started to swim immediately with their very similar breaststrokes, Anna almost but not quite matching her daughter's admirably strong style.

'We've swum in so many oceans and seas together, haven't we, Mum?'

'Loads. Let's see. We're swimming in the Atlantic, and we've swum in the Mediterranean.'

'And when we went to Greece with Flora we went in the Aegean, I think.'

'And the Caribbean Sea.'

'And the North Sea.'

The waves were just big enough to make both women work quite hard. They found themselves naturally going right around the massive rock to the other, more popular beach where the large 'Dor' was, turning their heads to each other so that they could be heard.

'You and Ben seem happy.'

'We are, Mum. Really happy.'

'And you don't feel too tucked away here? You don't miss London?'

Anna got a mouthful of seawater and spluttered a little.

'Not at all, Mum. The only thing I really miss about it is you and Dad. And Jason.'

They swam on in silence. It was a longer swim around the rock then she had first imagined. She was confident that they were both strong swimmers and so she didn't worry. She had taught Natasha herself. Taken her to the swimming pool every Sunday from when she was tiny.

'About Ben. I think he's the one, Mum. I really do.'

'Oh, and what does that mean?'

'Well, we're thinking about babies.'

Anna stopped and started to tread water.

'You're not pregnant are you?'

'Bloody hell, Mum. No, I'm not pregnant. I just wanted to tell you that we are thinking seriously about it. I thought you'd be happy. I know how much you love children and babies and stuff.'

Natasha stretched her neck far out of the water so that her mother could hear her and her words wouldn't be swallowed by the waves.

'But what about your teacher training?'

'Obviously I'm going to do that. I'm just saying in the next few years or so. Ben's twenty-eight, you see.'

Oh, Ben. They had to think about Ben now, did they?

'And you're not quite twenty-three.'

'Mum, how old were you when you had me?'

'I was twenty-three.'

'Well, I want to be a young mum like you.'

Anna started swimming again, kicking out violently behind her. She plunged down into the water and dived under the sea, ignoring the painful pressure on her ears. When she was underwater she opened her eyes and turned herself and looked above her to see her daughter's body moving through the sea, shafts of sunlight coming from between her legs. She tried to hold herself down there but felt her lungs needing to fill with air and pushed herself quickly to the surface.

'You all right, Mum? Sorry, I didn't mean to upset you. I thought you'd be pleased.'

Anna opened her eyes and felt the sting of the salt.

'Sorry, darling. Of course I'm pleased. I've got salt in my eyes, that's all.'

They swam, the light bouncing off the water so that it was hard to see ahead of them.

'Dad said that you'd been having a hard time.'

'Really? What did he tell you?'

'Nothing. He just said that you weren't your usual tough self. That you needed a break. That's all.'

They had almost swum round the rocks and the Dor was looming just beyond them. Anna estimated that they had been swimming for about three-quarters of an hour. She felt quite tired and was glad that the beach was in sight. Without even speaking, they decided to swim through the Dor, both women side by side, making their breaststrokes stronger by dipping their heads in the water. Just as they were both inside the arch a large wave came and push them from behind and up against the small, dagger-like rocks that jutted out on the side of the rock wall. Anna felt herself being thrown against something sharp and her knee was banged. She swallowed a large enough mouthful of water to make her feel as if she were choking.

Natasha, where was Natasha? She tried desperately to see around her what was happening, to open her eyes in the water and push her hair away. Where was she? Where was the daughter? As she did so, she felt a strong arm around her waist. She heard Natasha close to her, shouting into her ear; she felt her cheek against hers.

'Mum! Hold on to me. Put your arms around my neck.'

'Are you hurt, Natasha darling? Have you hurt yourself?'

It was hard to see through the confusion of the water and her hair falling down over her eyes.

'No, Mum. Have you?'

'I'm all right, love.'

Anna pushed off from the rock and both women swam as hard as they could so that they were not caught by the next swell. They both got to the beach at the same time and lay there on their stomachs laughing together. Natasha's dark curls stuck to her forehead, just as Anna could feel hers were doing. Then they both sat up in the shallow waters and looked out to the arch.

'We're completely mad going through the Dor. I'm so irresponsible. We were talking so much I didn't think. We just did it...'

Anna looked at her knee and saw that there was a small, deep gash in it. It looked like the sort of cut you got when you where a child and always falling into things. She cupped her hand and got some seawater and poured it so that the blood trailing down her leg was washed away for a moment.

'Mum, does your knee hurt?'

She was surprised to see David coming out of the sea, having to pull up his baggy, washed-out blue trunk. He looked furious.

'What the hell were you thinking of? Haven't you ever seen pictures of the Dor? It always has waves smashing up high against the rock; it's known to be bloody dangerous. The sea has to come through a tiny space. No one swims through it. Ever. Look: no one swimming through it. Most people would know that it's a mad thing to do. I was terrified watching you two getting smashed around.'

Natasha stood up and kissed her dad. Anna looked up at them, squinting. David stepped backwards into the water and carried on shouting at them both.

'I followed you round the rock. You were going at quite a pace. It was a bloody hard swim, that, and you two didn't seem to notice. I just saw you talking and talking... Oh, look, you've cut your knee, Anna.'

'Yes, but Natasha rescued me, didn't you Nat?'

'Hardly, Mum.'

'Yes, you did. I felt your arm around me and it was so strong. I didn't know you were so strong, darling.'

Natasha smiled at her mother and then looked up with her hand over her eyes and waved to Ben, who was coming down the steps cut into the stone down their side of the beach. All their bags and beach stuff weighed him down. Anna was glad. She didn't want to have to walk all the way along the shingled beach to get back to their camp.

'Don't come down. We're coming up. Just put the bags down and we'll come up!' Natasha shouted to him, so that the other families on the beach looked at them.

As she started to climb the steep stone steps, Anna felt a jolt of joy. She turned to look across the sea and at the Dor and saw a massive wave push itself through, splashing right up against the side of the rock. She felt proud and elated that she and her daughter had managed to swim though that. How mad and brave and strong they both were.

Summer of Seven
The official blog of Professor Horace Henderson
BA (Yale), MS, PhD (Cornell)
June 25th 2011

I knew that there would be food there and blankets and that I had a torch in my knapsack and we would be all right in there together, nothing could get at us in there. Uly tried to get me to agree that we would lie there longer and I gave him an apple and told him that it would give him energy for the last lap and that this was our adventure together and that we had to be tough.

Comments: 1

MrBojangles said:

Are you talking about your son or someone else?

Chapter 13

The next day Natasha had some marking to do and Ben needed to check the farm's water levels so Anna and David decided to take themselves off for a long walk. Soon they were heading along the cliff top, where underfoot the grass was bouncy and thick with clover. Without exchanging a word, they just kept going. They walked for hours, on and on, barely speaking, David setting the pace, Anna always behind. And then, all at once, she had had enough of him striding in front of her. Taking a deep breath, she ran past him.

'Oh no you don't,' he said, just as she came level with him. He grabbed hold of her and flung her shrieking to the ground. They were close enough to the edge of the cliff for her scream to be genuine. He lay on top of her. He glanced briefly to left and right. Winston stood by them, wagging his tail.

'Piss off!' David told the dog.

He kissed Anna hard. Overhead, the sun was blinding, so she could only squint up at him. He reached down to undo his zip. If a Labrador had not come bounding up at that precise moment and a woman had not called out from the distance, he would have put himself inside her. Instead they got up, both giggling. The woman, a serious walker in her long shorts and socks and sturdy boots and mountain walking sticks, came nearer. The Labrador ran back to her.

'Are you all right there? Is everything OK? I saw you both on the ground.'

They both laughed out loud. Like teenagers. Anna brushed herself down.

'We're fine but thanks for asking!' David shouted back at her across the cliff-top wind.

The woman suddenly realised what was going on. Her face turned thunderous as she walked away. But the moment had passed and they had seen themselves from the hiker's point of view. On they went in single file.

Later, they sat in the West Bay fish restaurant and devoured two lobsters, sucking the meat from sandpaper limbs, cracking them with their teeth and snapping them with their fingers. As they ate, Anna explained to David that she thought that Ben was one of those men who had a secret self revealed only to a woman he loved.

'You were a bit like that, David. When we first met. You were my secret. You didn't really speak to my friends but when we were alone in bed you would talk to me about everything. You would show me your private self and it was completely fascinating to me. A real surprise. Do you remember? You were all mine. None of it was bullshit to impress other people. You didn't seem to care what other people thought of you. Natasha and I don't go for men who are the centre of attention at parties, then retreat into silence in the car on the way home. We like the opposite. The opposite is better.'

She poured herself another glass of white wine.

David smiled, flushed with pleasure at her words.

'It was so strange the way the university's science and humanities departments were so unashamedly divided then. I wonder if it is still like that. The students didn't even have to walk past each other because the buildings were at the opposite ends of the campus. It was very rare to meet polyvelts.'

David laughed.

'Remind me why you called us polyvelts?'

'Don't you remember? The scientists were called that because of the beige, orthopaedic shoes they all wore. Almost moulded to their feet.'

Anna had been dancing in a club in Brighton, not caring who was looking at her, when suddenly there he was, staring right into her eyes. His long black hair, large nose, pale skin and dark caterpillar eyebrows singled him out from everyone else. His body was lean under his jeans and a white shirt that was slightly too small for him. She stopped dancing and moved a little closer to him. It was then that she saw, through the coloured lights, that he was wearing polyvelts. Black polyvelts instead of the usual hideous tan colour, but polyvelts all the same. Anna was young enough and shallow enough to reject him there and then because of his shoes.

'You wore polyvelts, David, don't you remember?'

He shrugged.

She explained again what they were.

'They sound great. Where can I get some?'

The next time she saw him, he was queueing at the campus bank, trying to write on his paying-in slip with one of those chained pens. She smiled at him and looked down at his feet and felt cheered that this time he was wearing some battered black Converse trainers with black, old-men's trousers. She remembered thinking they might have come from a charity shop. This was far more acceptable. Please look at me, she willed. Instead, she took her Bic pen from her back pocket and gave it to him. He used it and handed it back to her without a word.

Anna's obsession with David became a private joke between herself and her female friends. Anna fancied a polyvelt geek, rather than a boy with a quiff and a fifties checked shirt or with a shaved head and baggy clothing! She even started having lunch in the polyvelt canteen on the chance that she might bump into him.

The first time they had sex, his passionate, skilful lovemaking disarmed her. After that, they were together most of the time, staying awake in each others' arms all night and attending tutorials and lectures all day. For Anna, the company of a scientist was mysterious and impressive, his thoughts more precise and meticulous than any of her previous boyfriends.

She sucked the last bit of flesh from the lobster's claw and told him how impressed she had been by him. Then.

'Oh, don't say it in the past tense,' he said.

'Obviously I'm still very impressed by you. You're a very impressive man.'

He rubbed his foot up her leg under the table. 'I think you'd be very impressed by me right now.'

He smiled saucily at her. She noted how easy it was to make him happy.

Lying in bed the next morning, with the sun coming in the small cottage window through its flimsy floral curtains, they promised each other that when they got home, they would book a holiday in Sicily for three weeks. It would be the longest David had ever been away from the lab. Later, Anna went through to the tiny kitchen where Natasha and Ben were eating breakfast before they left for work. She stood in front of them.

'We've had a wonderful time, you two. Thanks so much.'

They smiled up at her.

'Do you want me to strip the beds for you?'

Anna looked at Ben sitting there so close to Natasha as they ate and thought that she had come round to him because he obviously adored Natasha. He had shown them round the watercress farm proudly and Anna had genuinely admired the concrete ponds bursting forth with the pretty, bright-green plants. They had eaten the peppery leaves most nights as a salad and Anna believed Natasha when she said that she thought the watercress had special properties.

'Don't worry. You don't have to take them off. Gran never does.' Natasha spoke with her mouth full, like David. Anna wondered if she had heard correctly.

'Gran?'

Natasha reddened. She looked as if she regretted what she had said. As if she wanted to retrieve the words and swallow them back. She took a sip of tea to hide her confusion. Anna watched as some of it dribbled out of her mouth. Then she swallowed too loudly.

'Sorry. Didn't I tell you? Gran has stayed here a few times. You know how she feels about the West Country.'

Anna couldn't believe that her mother had stayed here, in the same bed, in the same little house, before she had. Before she and David had. She tried to keep her composure but did not succeed. Mumbling something, she headed out of the door. The feeling of betrayal had taken her by surprise. Of course, she knew that Natasha and her grandmother got on well, but never had she imagined that they were that close.

Anna walked to the end of the garden and started to dead-head the rose that climbed up the wall separating the cottage from the immediate neighbours. She heard Natasha coming after her. She did not dare turn, not until she had regained control, because she was close to tears.

'Sorry, Mum. Are you really upset that Gran has stayed here? I don't quite get why?'

She turned to look at her daughter. Natasha's face was concerned but her voice was defensive. Anna felt even more foolish. She winced as a thorn went down her thumbnail. She sucked it, feeling its hard point with her tongue.

'Ignore me. I'm being an idiot. I didn't know you got on that well with her. It just feels a bit odd – her being here before us. That's all. It's stupid.'

Natasha stepped forward.

'I've always got on with Gran, Mum. You know I have... Both Jason and me find her... a laugh, I suppose. I know you have problems with her but you know how much easier it is for grandchildren to get on with their grandparents. I find her funny...'

Anna felt herself bristle. 'Funny? I've never noticed her being funny. She has never made me laugh. Not that I can remember. You know what she was like to me when I was a child. I've told you about how awful it was for me.'

Natasha's face became serious. 'Look, this is mad, Mum. We get a bit pissed together. She knows that she was a crap mother to you but she's so much better than most grandmothers. She doesn't interfere and I like that. She's not judgemental. I feel that she completely accepts me as I am, as a grown-up.'

Why did Anna feel that these words were an attack on her? Her thumbnail was throbbing, adding to the pain in her voice.

'I accept you as a grown-up.'

Natasha tried to smile.

'Mum, you don't. Not really.'

'Oh! Don't I?'

'I always feel with you that you're missing me so much as a little girl that you are missing out on me now. All those stories you tell me about how I was when I was young make me feel... well... I feel as if you are always trying to drag me back to a place I hardly remember. I feel a bit claustrophobic in your house with my room just as it always was. I know that Gran wasn't particularly interested in me as a child but now I'm grown up, she seems to really like me.'

Anna wanted to burst into tears and say how unfair it all was. After all, she had always put the children first because her own mother had never put her first. Now she was being told that her parenting was all wrong; that her daughter preferred her monster of a mother staying in the cottage. And Nat hadn't asked how she felt about being made redundant. She hadn't even mentioned it. No one thought her work was important. Maybe that was the message she had given out herself. She held back her tears but she could feel her mouth trembling and pulling down at the corners.

'You're right about me. I do miss both of you so much. And you're right about the room. You're probably right about the whole house.

As you often say, it's going to be far too big for us soon… and I lost my job.'

Natasha moved forward to embrace her.

'Come on, Mum. It's all right. Dad told me about the job. I didn't want to bring it up on your birthday in case I upset you. I was waiting for you to talk about it.'

There was a long pause. Neither seemed to have anything to add.

'And, you know, you have no reason to feel jealous of Gran. I know she's a selfish old witch, I really do. She doesn't have a maternal bone in her body.'

Anna put her arms round her daughter. She was comforted by those last words.

On the drive back home, she and David listened to sixties reggae. She told David what Natasha had said about wanting to have babies soon.

'Not right now, I hope. It's too soon. I don't want you becoming a professional grandmother.'

His remark irritated her but before she could respond, she felt her phone vibrate at her feet. She picked it up, expecting it to be Natasha. It was a text from a number she didn't recognise.

'Sad you walked out on me at the club. See me again please. Cup of coffee? Alphonse xx'

Anna snapped her phone shut.

Summer of Seven
The official blog of Professor Horace Henderson
BA (Yale), MS, PhD (Cornell)
June 26th 2011

Up until then, Uly and I had been doing just fine. By consulting the map we had been given, we had climbed up Brown John hill, found the food Father had left for us in the hollow of a big oak tree and then we had walked miles over the hills and across the valley. We were stopped only once by a man walking his dog. He asked us if we were lost. Uly wanted to ask him if he had some candy but I told him Father would be angry. I told the man we were fine and he waved us on our way.

Comments: 4

Ihatepanpipes said:
My four year old son has an imaginary friend. Last week he threw a toy bus at his baby sister and caused quite a serious bump on her head. When we told him off he said that "Dodi did it". He seems to really think that he shouldn't take responsibility. Is he too old to have an imaginary friend?

JeenieB said:
I am an ex-student of Professor Horace Henderson. He has always been a controversial, thought-provoking figure. I have carefully read each of his posts. I presume the comparison here is between the way he carefully monitors his son's progress in outdoor pursuits and his own father's dubious and arms-length parenting. He is encouraging his readers to compare his own parenting – careful guidance towards step-by-step independence – and his father's offhand, cold parenting which came from his inability to process his own grief. Interesting

stuff. I look forward to the publication of the collected blogs.

Mimmi said:

I now have an infant son of my own. I hope to raise him to be independent and that means letting him go places by himself when he is ready, just as my parents let me go places on my own. I don't want him to fear the world. I want him to live in it. After all, there will come a time when I won't be there to hold his hand, much as I may want to. If he can't hold his own, I will have failed as a parent. I am very glad that Professor Henderson is putting his theory into practice with his own child, not just telling other parents how to raise their children.

MrBojangles:

Please post pictures of your daily endeavours.

Chapter 14

It hadn't been hard to persuade Carol to accompany her to a talk by Professor Henderson at the Quaker Centre in the Euston Road. Carol's three children were under ten and Anna knew that she was an avid reader of parenting books. When Anna went round to pick her up, she let her in and then ran upstairs again to find her bag. Anna wandered into the kitchen and picked up one of the books piled on the table and flicked through it. *Poisoned Kids: How the Way We Live Damages our Children and What to Do About It.* It was a diatribe against producing slobby, rude, fat, ill kids by not obeying the book's rules. Its hectoring tone irritated her. The next one sounded better: *Parenting with Laughter.* It contained jolly cartoons, and was written in a jocular style with lots of exclamation marks. There were case studies of fun, family incidents in big italics. Anna put it down. It was worse than the first.

Carol returned, brushing her thick, blonde hair.

'There's some helpful stuff in those books. I was just looking through them to see if there was any roaming child stuff in preparation for tonight. I thought I had a Henderson book somewhere but I can't find it. I think I leant it to my bloody sister.'

Anna didn't say anything.

'I know that you should take it with a pinch of salt but if you mix and match, you come up with something useful. And I need all the help I can get.'

Carol had begun late and believed that all other parents were doing a better job than she was – she and her good-natured, red-faced husband. It surprised Anna how little confidence had spilled over from her high-powered job in PR into her parenting. Anna found herself in the role of counsellor: currently it was over the six-year-old who refused to go to bed and whether the nine-year-old was safe walking to the newsagents. Her advice was valued only because her children were safely grown up without anything terrible having happened to them, not because she was considered a particularly good mother. Anna usually came up with something that sounded plausible to both of them, but she actually had no idea whether she had let her children go to the corner shop or the swings when they were nine or if she had waited until they were a bit older.

'Why are you interested in going tonight, Anna?' Carol asked, once they were on their way in Anna's car. 'I thought you'd never read a parenting book in your life. And why Horace Henderson? I know he was really, really popular a couple of years ago. I think he was the first to start talking about kids being allowed to explore beyond their own gardens.'

'Yes, I know that, only he's just moved in opposite my mother.' Anna had a vision of Henry's terrified face as he flew through the air on the swing. She tried to concentrate on her driving. 'Anyway, I knew this would entice you out.'

She glanced at Carol while changing gears and thought how lovely she still was. Her thick, blonde fringe, in need of a cut, nearly covered her eyes and made her look like a sulky teenager. Her black silk shirt, once expensive, had a suspicious white stain near the breast area. Anna remembered buying that shirt with Carol in Marylebone Road, in her lunch hour, twelve or so years ago, when she was still working at the agency. She had been jealous that Carol looked so tall and rangy.

'I do think his ideas about a free-roaming child are interesting, particularly now that Sam is ten. I don't know what I should be letting him do. I'm in such a muddle. I find myself disapproving of parents who let their children do too much and too little! Most mothers act intuitively, whereas I rarely feel confident with my own decisions.'

'You're doing fine, Carol. Your kids always seem lovely. Sam comes and talks to me in such a grown-up way. He remembers the names of my kids and the dog. He looks at me when I speak to him. That's so unusual.'

Carol pushed her floppy fringe out of her eyes.

'You don't think it's too unusual?'

'No.'

'Do you think he is one of those kids who can only relate to grown-ups?'

'Well, does he have friends of his own age?'

'Yes. Loads. Oddly enough, he's always been very popular.'

'Why's that odd?'

'Because he is pretty eccentric, I think.'

'What do you mean?'

Carol looked at her and hesitated. Perhaps she felt disloyal to Sam.

'Well, he has rituals that I help him with before he goes to sleep.'

'Like what?'

'Straightening the curtain, pushing the bed in, looking under the bed, going through the names of everyone he loves.'

'Is that all? Before she would go to sleep, Natasha would make me list the names of everyone in the family and answer as if I was them. Including the pets. Including the tropical fish. I made tropical fish noises.'

Carol laughed 'What noise was that then?'

'Like a goldfish noise but more exotic.'

Anna made the noise and Carol laughed until tears poured down her cheeks.

'Oh heavens, what a relief! It's so good to know that. It's so good to talk about the things I worry about. John thinks I'm fussing and switches off.'

'They all have their rituals. It's instead of saying your prayers, isn't it? The Victorian child used to find that reassuring. I suppose it was a way of setting everything in order before going to sleep. That's how I used to think of it, anyway.'

Carol smiled. 'They are all eccentric. Perhaps that's what being a child is about. Being yourself before you modify your behaviour to fit in with what is acceptable.'

'Everything you've described seems well within the range of normality,' Anna said.

'Good.'

'I'm not dismissing the way you feel about the children. I know how hard it is, particularly when you have all this stuff telling you what to do.'

'What do you mean?'

'Well, I hear all these mothers with controlled voices that some parenting group has told them to use explaining like mad to their three-year-old in the midst of a tantrum why they have to leave the playground. Sometimes I don't think it hurts to just give the kid a fireman's lift and take them out of that supermarket and just be angry, if you feel like it. Why pretend to be calm and rational when you want to scream?'

'So it would be better to scream at them?'

'Sometimes it would.'

'Oh, I don't know.'

Carol started fiddling with the bag on her lap. She fished out her mobile and checked it for messages from home. Having been reassured by Anna, she seemed to have suddenly lost confidence in her.

'Sorry, Carol. I'm telling you what to do when really I have no idea. Natasha was a nightmare when she was a teenager. She made me feel like I was the worst parent in the world. There was one parents' evening when she told me, in from of the geography teacher, that I was a bitch! At the time, I felt she would never change. She would always hate me.'

'Did she really do that?' Carol smiled. 'I think Nat is so lovely.'

Anna parked the car down a side road close to the station and the two women crossed the Euston Road. At the door to the hall, Anna had a moment of panic. She had tried to change her appearance so that the Professor would not recognise her – her curly hair was scraped back into a tight bun, she wore glasses instead of her usual contacts and she had put on some bright-red lipstick that had once belonged to Natasha. She wanted to watch him without him noticing her. She wanted to take a long, hard look at him while he was speaking.

The entrance hall was already crowded. Two women sat behind a long trestle table where Henderson's more popular books were piled high. Anna handed over a twenty-pound note for two tickets.

'Can I ask how you heard about Professor Henderson's talk tonight?' the woman asked.

'On the Internet, I think.'

'Really? Most of the people here were invited through their Skills4Parents groups.'

'I can't really remember how. Sorry. Does it matter?'

The woman looked at her for a moment.

'It's just that we would like to know for our records.'

Anna immediately took a dislike to this woman, with her strawberry blonde hair and sandy eyebrows. And someone had obviously done her the disservice of telling her to wear heavy green eye shadow to compliment her colouring.

'Well, I can't remember.'

'That's fine. The more the merrier. Could you just sign here? We like to have the names of everyone. It's useful for us.'

Anna hesitated, then signed. When Carol bent over to add her name, she gave Anna a very quizzical look.

'Jane Bunting?' she asked, as they walked into the hall.

'I like to retain my mystery. I don't see why they have to know who I am. That sandy woman irritated me. It was an invasion of my privacy.'

'She was just doing her job. She probably wants you to join the parent group she mentioned and send you emails about their important work.'

'Maybe they want to check that everyone here believes in the roaming child theory?'

'Forget my children, Anna! You're the one who's becoming eccentric. Who's Jane Bunting, anyway?'

'I don't know. A girl who used to sit next to me in French? A character in a girl's comic? A young Tory MP? I don't know. It just came to me.'

The seats in the hall were arranged in a tiered semi-circle. Anna decided that she wanted to be in the middle, where she would be least conspicuous. Carol followed her, nodding on her way to a few parents whom she knew.

Finally everyone was settled and the sandy women, wearing a turquoise patterned tunic, got up on stage. Anna loathed 'fun' clothes on grown women.

'Good evening, Thank you all so much for coming. I'm Ruth Franklin from Skills4Parents UK.'

There was muted clapping.

'This is the second in our series of talks from parenting experts and I know a great many of you are particularly excited about this one. He needs no introduction. It's a great, great honour to have with us, from the United States, the originator of the 'Roaming Free' parenting movement. Can we give a very warm welcome to Professor Horace Henderson!'

Professor Henderson jogged on to the stage and stood in front of the lectern. His height and mane of hair gave him an other-worldly look, like a slightly mad conductor. The audience clapped again, more enthusiastically, and Carol nudged her. 'Come on. Join in,' she whispered. 'He's impressive looking, isn't he?'

'I suppose so.'

Anna made herself clap a couple of times. If only Carol knew what she knew. Professor Horace Henderson terrorised and neglected his own child. He was a liar.

The Professor went straight to asking the audience a question – American style. No messing about with preambles.

'How many of you like watching wildlife programmes?'

People around Anna nodded and made small sounds in the backs of their throats – British style – to imply that they did indeed enjoy watching wildlife programmes. A woman in front of Anna half-raised her hand and then put it down quickly when she noticed that no one else had done so.

'Do you enjoy it when you see a film of young chimpanzees rolling around with each other? Leaping from tree to tree, tasting new things, trying new things, learning from their experience? Do you know why you enjoy it so much? Well, here's why. Because you know, somewhere in your hearts, that in order to develop, to learn the physical control and co-ordination those chimps will need to survive, to become properly formed, functioning adults, they need to go through the joyous rough and tumble of play and they need to take a few risks, perhaps even step over the line and take a few knocks and bruises and maybe a couple of cuts. It's a beautiful thing to watch, isn't it?'

More strangled but appreciative sounds from the audience. They knew where they were being led but they were thoroughly enjoying it.

'OK, you all agree that watching young chimpanzees playing is a beautiful thing, so I'd like to ask you a question, if I may?'

You've already asked two questions, Anna thought grumpily. She hated the falsely modest 'if I may' when it was obvious he was just going to go ahead and ask his damn question anyway. Anna had a strong intuition that she was the only person in the audience who felt the slightest objection.

'So, why do you bind your kids up in bubble-wrap?'

A meaningful pause. This was, after all, the crux of the matter.

'Why deprive them of those trial-and-error experiences? You all know instinctively that this is the way our own young learn fundamental physical, social and emotional lessons. Gradually, and for a number of reasons related to modern civilisation, you have deprived your children of these essential experiences which will help them grow into healthy, non-dependent adults.'

Henderson never raised his voice. He knew his words were powerful enough. People were nodding their heads in agreement, some vigorously. He continued. He listed the ways in which parents were going badly wrong: children being driven to school, children leading sedentary, screen-based lifestyles, children being taken to theme-based parks which killed their imaginations. He went on to tell his audience that the ordinary adventure had been eradicated by frightened parents who controlled their children.

'By "ordinary adventure", I mean those small but significant moments in which children learn about the world and find opportunities to take risks, make judgments, to learn how to make friends and deal with enemies.'

Then Henderson paused, allowing his audience to assimilate what he had just said. When he started speaking again, his tone had changed.

'One fall... autumn to you Brits...' he began, as if letting the audience into a secret, 'a group of boys used to wait for me after school to throw chestnuts at me. I believe you call them conkers. I was an OK baseball player, so do you know what I did? I just took my Little League baseball bat and hit those chestnuts away. They kept on raining down on me but I kept on hitting them back. Needless to say, the bullying stopped. The boys and I became pretty good friends. Do you know why? I had worked out the best way to survive and at an instinctive level, they knew that. I didn't ask my dad. I worked it out for myself.'

Smug bastard, Anna thought. But the appreciative audience smiled and laughed.

'Another time, there was a big oak tree that I couldn't climb because I was the smallest. Yeah, I know it's hard to imagine me being small.'

Ha, ha, laughter all around. A bit of light self-mockery was another way to get his audience on side.

'All the other boys climbed it but I couldn't make it even to the first branch. Then I noticed a tyre in the ditch and even though I was only six or seven years old and it was very heavy, I rolled it slowly to that tree and pushed it right against the trunk. Yes, you've guessed the ending.' More laughter. 'The tyre gave me a leg up and soon I was climbing to the very top of the tree. I will never forget that feeling. Never forget what it was like to look down from the top branches. There was no parent there to suggest or to tell me what to do. No parent to oversee and control what I did. There was no belittling of the experience.'

He stood up, stepping slightly away from the lectern, and pushed his grey mane back with a dramatic sweep of his hand.

'And there was another bonus, besides the sense of achievement. Playing outside, I learnt about nature and birds and insects. I learnt that some plants were sticky enough to cling to the backs of other boys. I learnt that I could give myself a tattoo out of the juice of a dandelion flower. I learnt that when I pressed a fern on the back of my hand, it left a beautiful white spidery imprint. What magical moments they were!'

All around her, people looked enraptured. They held their breath while he was speaking and let it out in a rush of admiration and agreement now that he had finished. Everyone, it seemed, except

Anna.

Had he finished? Anna wondered if they were meant to get up and leave now, but no one was moving. Then she saw a group of women moving quietly down the aisles, handing out pieces of paper and pencils. While they did this, Henderson leant again towards his microphone, his voice even softer than before, and husky. She could hear his heavy breathing. Wasn't this what stage hypnotists did? This man knew exactly what he was doing. She could not fault his performance.

'May I ask you to do a little something for me? Do you mind taking a few minutes to write down a childhood experience? Something that had nothing to do with your parents. Just something spontaneous and joyful that took place outdoors. Can everyone manage that? When you have finished, we will put all the accounts in a hat and I'll read out five of them. Just to remind us all what it is like to be a free-range child.'

Carol was scribbling away with enthusiasm.

'What are you writing?' Anna asked.

'I don't know. Maybe about the time my brothers lowered me into the hollow of a tree. They wanted to upset me but I quite liked it. It was peaceful away from them, sitting in the mushroomy, knobbly half-dark, waiting for them to come back.'

'Did they pull you out eventually?'

'I think they left me in there for quite a long time, maybe until supper time when Mum noticed that I wasn't there. They were punished. But I still remember how quiet it was in the tree and how safe I felt and how I liked looking at the garden out of one of the tiny holes, knowing that no one could see me. I became a tree-girl. I was part of the tree.'

'I can see why you might like that'

'What about you? What are you going to write?'

'Oh… I don't think I'll write anything…'

'Why not? Come on! Everyone else is.'

Anna folded her arms. One of the official women with a therapeutic smile arrived at their aisle.

'You know, while you don't have to write a memory, we really do encourage everyone to have a go at writing about a childhood experience.'

'What if I don't remember any "roaming experiences"?'

'You only need to write a couple of lines. Just enough to bring back memories of being free as a child.'

People turned to stare at Anna. She could see that Henderson was chatting to the woman who had introduced him. The last thing she wanted was to draw attention to herself, so she mumbled that she would have a go. Slowly, reluctantly, she wrote about Somerset, irritated that she was giving Henderson one of her memories, but it would have taken more effort to invent one. At the end of her short story, she left a space and added, in smaller, slightly scrawled writing: Your son is not an experiment. Take better care of him. Please! She thought it highly unlikely that her piece of paper would be chosen – but she desperately wanted to tell him that she knew what he was.

The pieces of paper were collected in several buckets. Back on the stage, each was tipped into one huge one. Henderson bent over the microphone again, his smooth voice oiling the audience into willing awe and gratitude. He was shaking the bucket and smiling.

He laughed and said that it was a lucky dip of magical memories and thanked everyone for their contributions. Did each member of the audience feel the same balance of hope and dread?

He read out the first story about a girl taking a pony out without supervision and riding bareback. The second one was about sliding down a mudbank into a river and then rolling deliberately in grey mud. They were enjoyable in a light, harmless sort of way. He put his hand in the bucket for the third.

'I was an only child. I always longed to stay with my grandparents in Somerset.'

Anna heard herself inhale sharply.

'There was a massive hay barn next to the house that was used by the elderly farmer who owned the fields around them. One day, my cousins and I decided that if we carefully pushed out some of the bales of hay, we could make a tunnel from one end of the hay barn to the other. We did it and crawled through. Of course it was stupid. The whole thing could have collapsed and buried us. But it didn't. Making that tunnel was one of the best days I can remember.'

Then he stopped. He peered at the piece of paper. He looked around the room. He leant against the lectern and glared into the audience. Was he going to single her out and point at her? She would probably be lynched by this crowd of Henderson worshippers. There was a slight murmuring around her. The audience sensed something was wrong. The woman who had made the effusive introduction climbed back up on the stage and stood on her tiptoes to speak in the Professor's ear.

He bent down to her height, told her something and put Anna's note into his pocket. Carol whispered, 'I was just getting into that.'

'It was mine.'

'Oh my God! Well done. You got picked.' Carol turned to her friend and beamed.

On stage, Professor Henderson seemed to have abandoned the anecdotes and had returned to his thesis.

'You know, a guy called Tacitus from ancient Greece has something important to say on this subject. He knew that it was part of a father's duty to train his boys and girls in survival skills. Let me tell you a bit about the Spartans, because they have got a bad press. In fact, the Greeks themselves held the fathering techniques of the Spartans in high regard. It was not all about exposing weak babies on hillsides, you know.'

As he spoke, he stared intently at his audience, moving his eyes from row to row. His voice was more animated and forceful. Anna saw a spray of spit fly from his mouth.

'We could all take something from the Spartan way of thinking and understand that a child needs to rely on his own resources from an early age, and should be inspired to dig deep and find the very best in himself. He has the right to avoid protection and suffocation. He has the right to build his own strength. From within.'

He paused.

'This is what the Oracle of Delphi said to Lycurgus, the Regent of Sparta, who wrote the Spartan constitution: There are two roads, most distant from each other: the one leading to the honourable house of freedom, the other to the house of slavery, which mortals must shun. It is possible to travel the one through manliness and lovely accord; so lead your people to this path. The other they reach through hateful strife and cowardly destruction; so shun it most of all.'

He looked out at them intently, his voice booming out. 'The muscles of children's bodies have become slack with misuse – with being folded up in front of screens all day. You are turning your children into flabby slobs whose imaginations have been hijacked by murderous computer games!'

Strong stuff. At first, as if stunned, the audience barely responded. Then the clapping began, and escalated, as people woke from their trance. The men were on their feet, whooping and cheering. A woman close to Anna was softly sobbing.

Professor Henderson responded with an encore, like a musician acknowledging the credit bestowed on him.

'Let your children climb the highest tree without worrying that they will fall! Allow them unsupervised time every now and then! Make the most of your wonderful city with so many parks. Take them out into the countryside. Nature offers tests all the time, wherever you look. Let them grow into adults who have confidence and magnificence! Let your children be free!'

He was about to make his exit when the sandy woman whispered in his ear.

'Oh yes, Ruth has just reminded me to tell you about my blog site called The Summer of Seven. The official blog of Horace Henderson. It's a personal record of how I am setting my own son free. Some of you might be interested.'

By now, she wanted only one thing – to get out as quickly as possible. She tried to steer Carol though the front doors but her friend made a beeline for the book stall, where Professor Henderson himself was holding forth, surrounded by excited, admiring women and a couple of men. They all held pens up to him. He was a whole head taller than anyone else and Anna saw that in between ducking down to sign books, he was carefully watching the crowd.

'Oh, I must buy a book and get it signed.'

Carol's face was flushed and excited.

'I'll meet you back at the car. I'm not feeling very well. I just need a bit of fresh air. You go ahead.'

Carol turned to her, puzzled.

'Do you want me to come with you?'

'No. You go ahead. You remember where the car is? By the British Library in that side street.'

But Carol had already turned away and was in the slipstream of people on their way to the Professor. Anna pushed through the crowd and left the hall. Taking big gulps of the fume-filled air of Euston Road, she walked briskly back towards the car. Only once she was alone and had the doors locked was she was able to steady her breathing. Why had she been so stupid? That comment had been lunacy. And yet, although she had frightened herself, part of her was glad that she, at least, had cut through some of the Henderson crap.

She had let him know that in that cheering, sycophantic crowd, there was one person who was on to him.

Summer of Seven
The official blog of Professor Horace Henderson
BA (Yale), MS, PhD (Cornell)
July 1st 2011

Characteristics Of A Female Stalker:

Her behavior is often triggered initially by the end or the winding down of a relationship, most commonly with a romantic partner, but also with an estranged mother, a close friend, or even with a child. Often, these "rejected" stalkers experience ambivalent feelings which are a complex mixture of reconciliation and revenge. Sometimes they convince themselves that their love is requited and even when they recognize that their love is not returned, they insist with delusional intensity on both the legitimacy and the eventual success of their quest.

Comments: 52

Daveyboy said:

Not sure I understand any of your posts so far but can I just say how inspirational your talk was tonight. It really took me back to my own childhood and all the rough and tumble I enjoyed. It made me so sad to realise how little of that adventure my own children have had. I am determined to try and let go, to allow them to be part of their own world.

SarahK said:

I was wondering if you could possibly advise me? My son is nine years old and wants to walk to school on his own. It is only a twenty minute walk. Do I let him? The other mothers in the playground have expressed horror that I am even thinking of it.

Dflavar said:

Your son should have been walking to school by himself for at least two years! As Prof H would say stop this bubble wrapping!!

Kidsneedads:

How refreshing your talk was with it's robust defence of a father's important role in a child's life. I think you will agree that it is time that mothers stopped dominating the parenting agenda and the legal systems of the UK and US. I wondered if you would be interested in talking to a Kidsneedads conference in December of this year?

Doorstepwoman said:

Your son is not an experiment.

Read more...

CHAPTER 15

The next Sunday Anna waited on the path for five minutes. Then she turned the corner and walked right up to the swimmers' entrance to the pond. There was Henry, talking to a young man whose hand rested casually on the gate behind him. From the awkward way he held his head and from the *blink, blink,* Anna knew that Henry didn't know this person. She ran, Winston close at heel.

'Henry!'

Henry looked up and moved so close that his wet hair seeped through her cotton dress on to her skin. Anna put her arm around his shoulder and turned to the man.

'Can I help you?'

The man looked defensive. He put his hand on his chin and rubbed the bristle, making a horrible rasping sound.

'I was just speaking to the boy. He didn't seem to have anyone with him.'

'Well, now he does. Me.' Henry moved even closer and leaned into her hip.

The man looked her up and down. She remembered her own encounters on the heath when strange men would try to start up an ordinary conversation with her – about the weather or the time – before asking her, out of the blue, if she would just hold their thingies while they did a pee.

'We've got to get going. Goodbye, now.'

Anna took hold of Henry's cold little hand. He took it away quickly.

"What's the matter Henry?"

He still carried on looking down. He spoke in a mumble. She had to lean down to him to hear it.

"Nothing." He shrugged.

"Come on. What is it?"

He looked up at her, blinking hard.

"You said you would come and see me last Sunday. I was looking for you and Winston but you weren't there. Dad kept asking me who I was looking for."

"I'm so sorry, Henry. It was my birthday. I went to visit my daughter in Dorset. It was a surprise."

She exaggerated the surprise part of it because children love a birthday surprise. He looked up, his curiosity getting the better of him.

"Really? You didn't know you were going? Who did the surprise for you?"

"Well, my husband and my daughter arranged it. We drove to my daughter's cottage, quite near the sea."

"Did you take Winston?"

"Yes. Winston came with us."

"Did he like the sea?"

"We couldn't let him go in the sea. There are some beaches where dogs aren't allowed at this time of year."

Henry looked genuinely cast down.

"Oh poor Winston. That's not fair. I think that Winston would like the sea."

"We have taken him to the sea before and he goes mad. He barks at the sea and pushes up the sand with his nose and runs around like crazy. You are allowed to take him on beaches in the winter. In the winter he can do what he likes."

Henry smiled when she said that Winston barked at the sea.

"What are those?"

"Oh, these are a pair of my son's shoes. When he was your age, he used to wear them in the summer. You remember I told you about my son Jason who was into dinosaurs too? He's in the jungle at the moment. Do you want to see if they fit you?"

Henry hesitated.

"I don't know."

"Well, it doesn't matter. It's just that you said that you stubbed your toes and cut them sometimes. You don't have to wear them. I can put them back in my bag."

Without a word, Henry sat down on the grass verge and stuck out his feet. She smiled and put on the jellies. He stood up and looked down at the clear red plastic sandals. They were only a little bit too big.

"Jason used to like them because you can go in the water with them and they don't get ruined."

"I like them."

"Good."

"Maybe you should take them off before we get home though."

Anna nodded. "You know when I first met you...when you said your father had hidden your shoes..."

"That's what Dad told me to say. That we had hidden them when we went swimming and had forgotten where."

Anna was appalled but tried not to show it. For a while they walked on in silence.

'By the way what did that man at the pool say to you?'

'He asked me if I liked swimming with my clothes off. He told me that it was his favourite way of swimming.'

'Oh, for God's sake! What a really silly, silly man. Don't speak to strangers, please. Don't you know that you shouldn't do that? Haven't your parents ever told you?'

Henry looked up at her.

'No. They haven't.'

His brow was furrowed and his lip stuck out. Maybe he thought that she was telling him off.

'Sorry, Henry. I didn't mean to sound cross. It's just that I was worried. I don't want anything to happen to you. Do you understand?'

He looked at her, his eyelashes still wet from his swim and separated into clumps.

'Well, I spoke to *you*. I didn't know you before I spoke to you, did I?'

He was right, of course, but it was difficult to think of herself as having been a stranger and that a few weeks ago, she had not even met him.

'Well, I'm different. Promise me that if someone tries to stop you like that, you will just walk on as if you didn't hear. Don't be polite and think you have to answer. Just walk away. If an adult wants to know something, he can ask another adult, can't he?'

Henry nodded his head. They walked on.

'I suppose you are doing even more things on your own now that it's the holidays?'

Another nod.

'Well, just remember what I've said. OK?'

'OK.'

'Promise? Otherwise I'll worry about you.'

'I promise, Anna.'

Anna kissed him on his wet head. Just a quick kiss. He didn't seem to notice.

'Thanks, Henry. Thanks, darling. Good boy.'

These brief early-morning encounters with Henry became part of Anna's daily routine. Afterwards, they would go to the swings or straight back to the Goldblatts' house – after Anna had removed Henry's shoes and left him to walk up Willowfield Road barefoot and alone. For a while she felt that everything was under control.

The following Saturday morning, though, Henry told Anna that he was to meet his dad somewhere else. He took Anna's hand and led her towards the woods beyond the swing. Anna loved the feel of his small damp hand, pulling her to a place she didn't know. An adult being led by a child. She tripped over roots and packed-down leaves as they walked downhill, deep into the dark hollow – a secret place unknown to the crowds that flocked to the heath every summer. He looked up at her.

'Careful. This is where I usually stub my toes but now I don't. These shoes help me go even faster down here. Look! I can nearly run down.'

Henry set off downhill at breakneck speed. Anna followed, trying to hang on to him to stop him from falling.

'Whoa! Careful there, Henry.'

Henry stopped at a pile of sticks and leaves that looked like someone had started to build a bonfire. He pulled off some of the sticks.

'Come on, Anna. Help me.' He was already out of breath with the effort.

Anna saw that beneath the casually arranged sticks was a skillfully woven construction. He looked up at her as if to ask her opinion.

'Oh! So your dad made you a secret house? Is that what it is?' Her first instinct was to admire its careful intricacy. Henry shrugged.

'We've been working on this together after school. Dad wouldn't let me play with my best friend, Faris, because his mum lets him watch TV and play computer games and that would distract me from this. We collect long, thin, bendy sticks to make the criss-cross walls.'

'Criss-cross walls?'

'That's what Dad calls them. Criss-cross walls. I've got my own knife to do cutting. Look!'

From his pocket he took a small folded knife with a wooden handle. He pulled out the sharp blade to show her.

'Gosh!' Anna was shocked. 'Aren't you are a bit young to be using a knife like that?'

He rolled his eyes at her. She had never seen him do that before.

'It's fine. I'm really good with knives. Dad taught me.'

'Oh. OK, then.'

He flicked the knife back into its case. Anna enjoyed this first rebellion against her. He was relaxed enough to disagree with her. To be himself.

'Do you want to come inside?'

'How do I get in?' Anna couldn't see an entrance.

'Well, you have to lift off the top and then we get in and pull it back down – like a roof.'

Anna noticed that each small joint had been tied with twine, making a strong interlocking structure. It was rather beautiful. Henry climbed in, white lines etched on the backs of his legs from the sharp ends of the sticks. There was rush matting on the floor. An orange, half a baguette and a flask had been left on it. The light from the twig walls made zigzag patterns on the floor.

'Come in, Anna.'

'I think I'm too big.'

'Please come in. I'd like it if you did.'

She looked in at Henry looking up at her. He usually asked nothing from her. Perhaps his slight resistance over the knife wasn't a sweet and natural rebellion but a sign that his father had got to him.

'Do you always keep food in here?'

'Yes. Dad always leaves food for me. Come in please, Anna.'

Anna stepped inside, one leg, then the other, the blood pumping in her ears. She really didn't want to do this.

'Now sit down and make yourself small so that you fit in.'

Anna did as she was told.

'Now pull the roof down and we'll be in our nest.'

'What did you call it?'

'Dad calls it a nest.'

'Do we have to pull the roof down? I'd prefer if it were left up. You see, I don't really like small spaces that much.'

Henry ignored her and pulled it down. As he did, he smiled slyly.

Winston was whining outside. Anna sat down and tried to make her body into a ball. Henry stuck his fingers through a slat to tickle the dog's nose.

'Sorry, Winston, but there's no room for you as well.'

Her legs and back felt cramped. She pushed back the panic.

'Won't your dad come along in a minute and find me here?'

Sweat dripped down her back.

'He said I was to sit and wait for a while on my own in the nest.'

'Why?' Anna's voice was sharp with anxiety.

'I'm not sure. I think to get used to it.'

'Why do you need to get used to it?'

Henry sighed at Anna's questioning. 'He just told me I had to wait in here.'

'But why?'

'To prepare for something.'

'To prepare for what?'

'I can't tell you.'

Ah, but she knew. And she had to get out. Henderson had got Henry to lure her into this woven cage so that he could trap her. To punish her for disrupting his lecture and for her comments on his mad blog. She felt her heart pumping . Breathing became a conscious effort, as if she had forgotten the simple in and out of it.

'I'm sorry, Henry. I have to get out. I'm finding it hard to breathe in here.'

Anna tried to stand.

Henry said again, 'I've got to wait here.'

Anna climbed out, scratching her legs. She wasn't going to wait around for Henderson. Not for one moment longer. Winston barked with delight.

She bent down and spoke into the cage, holding up the roof.

'I'll see you tomorrow, sweetie. I'll just hide somewhere for a few minutes. Make sure your dad comes.'

She took a deep breath to pull herself together and put Winston on the lead. Once she was breathing steadily again, Anna found a wide-spreading tree and stood behind it. A couple of times she shouted to Henry to ask if he was OK. He said he was, in his bravest voice. Anna wondered what he was thinking, sitting there alone. If she were to follow her instincts, she would lift him out and take him home. Why did he have to go through this?

And just when she was about to step forward, there he was. Henderson. Standing outside the cage. Shouting something at Henry. There were faint replies from inside the twig house but she couldn't hear what he was saying. She moved off then, walking so fast that she was at the pond almost before she realised it. She had been thinking so hard.

'Damn!' she said out loud. That bloody cage. Her fear had made her careless. She had forgotten to remove Jason's red jelly sandals from Henry's feet.

Summer of Seven
The official blog of Professor Horace Henderson
BA (Yale), MS, PhD (Cornell)
July 3rd 2011

Father had set up the rope swing from the sycamore tree. It had a branch which hung over the ravine, which was a dried up river bed. We could have scrambled down it but Father thought it would be exhilarating and challenging for us to swing across it. I went first and made it easily across to the other side but my heart had been in my mouth. I shouted back that it was easy. I wanted to let Uly know that he could do it too. I stood there, watching, waiting for Uly to take his turn. I think I shouted across the river bed, "Just grab the rope and you'll swing across to me, and I will be here to catch you."

Comments: 20

SarahK said:
What happened? Is this a true story? Please tell us what happened.

Stargazer said:
I love the way you illustrate your child-rearing theories with these narratives. I am a student of psychology at Bristol University and wondered if it would be possible to interview you about the effects of paternal distance on the under fives?

MissFunnypenny said:
My fourteen year old daughter wants to go to a festival on her own this summer. Do you think that is a good idea?

Janet B said:
My son still sucks his thumb at seven years old. Do you have a good method to stop him? I really don't like the idea of putting something

foul tasting on his thumb.

MrBojangles said:

What happened to your own adventures with your son. I don't understand where you are going with this and you still haven't replied directly to me.

Read more…

CHAPTER 16

Anna's mother was speaking so loudly on the other end of the phone that Anna had to hold it away from her ear.

'I'm very busy, Mum. I can't talk for long.'

'Sorry. I realise that you're terribly important and busy but could you come over tonight?'

'I'm not important. I don't have a job anymore. I don't think I told you.'

'What did you do?'

'Oh, I don't think it was my fault, Mum. People are being laid off everywhere.'

'Oh, I suppose they are. So you have lots of time on your hands now.'

'Well, I'm hoping to get freelance work again and I'm going to make Nat's room into a study so that I can work from home, so it could be a blessing in disguise.'

'Right. So you are going to do your little articles again.'

'Yes, Mum.'

'Well, I would really appreciate it if you popped round.'

'OK. What time?'

She wasn't in the mood to visit her mother, but she hoped that she might catch a glimpse of Henry at his window. Henry hadn't been at the pond for three mornings. The fear that he had been punished for the jelly shoes kept her awake at night.

Her mother's warm, uncomplicated welcome on the doorstep should have made her suspicious but she was preoccupied with her wish to look across the road into what she presumed was Henry's bedroom. Without saying anything, she started to climb the stairs. Her mother followed closely behind her.

'That's right. Go into the sitting room. There's someone there to see you, darling.'

Anna stopped and turned and looked down at her mother on the landing below. She only used that term of endearment when she was trying to impress someone. Anna noticed that her mother's short red hair had been smoothly sculptured over her small scalp and that she wore eye make-up and that her lips were as shiny as a teenage girl's. And so with a sense of dread, Anna walked into the upstairs sitting room and saw Henderson. She couldn't prevent herself from gasping. He looked up at her, a trace of a smile on his face.

'Hello, Anna. I think it's about time we talked, don't you?'

Anna felt her mother guiding her from behind towards the floral-patterned sofa opposite the Professor. She did as her mother wanted – like a child on her best behavior. 'Please sit down, Anna,' the Professor said.

Anna's mother placed herself on a wooden chair next to Henderson, so that Anna, when she was seated, was facing them both.

'Do you want to talk to me about what's being going on?' His voice was soft but firm. Her mother coughed very softly, her hand covering her mouth. She didn't usually cover her mouth.

'What do you mean?' Her heart was thudding in her chest.

'Henry has told me everything, Anna. He had no choice after I found the shoes on his feet. He's told me about the meetings in the mornings, the piggybacks, the dinosaur chat.'

'Well…' Anna paused, wanting to say so much but wary and very much on her guard. 'If you mean, am I worried about the way you're treating your son, then yes I am. I do worry about him. I'm worried about him now because I haven't seen him for a couple of days.'

Henderson's face remained stony.

'How old are your children, Anna?'

'Eighteen and twenty-two. Why? What has that got to do with Henry?'

Her voice was becoming shrill, despite her attempt to remain outwardly calm.

'And what sort of mother were you, would you say?'

She refused to reveal how intimidated she felt, so she tried to match his voice – cold and calm.

'I don't know. I don't know how to answer that. They seem to have turned out all right. I'm very proud of them. We all are. Aren't we, Mum?'

Her mother didn't look at her.

'Your mother tells me that you had a very difficult period with Natasha. Sometimes she used to scream and swear at you. And Jason went through a stage when he took drugs. Is that right?'

'Oh, for God's sake! What is this? It was a totally normal teenage stage for both of them. David and I handled it fine, thanks. It's very disloyal and wrong of my mother to say anything different.'

Anna looked at her mother, who was looking down. Her trim ankles were neatly folded, one over the other.

'Do you feel that your mothering is none of my business?' Everything he said was measured, as if he had prepared each sentence. Each question. And had predicted her responses.

'Well, yes. Yes, I do, actually. In fact, it's none of your bloody business. I don't know why you think you can talk to me like this.'

She saw his slow, deliberate smile. He left two leisurely beats before he said, 'So why is it any of your business how I parent my son, Anna?'

This time Anna allowed herself to pause before giving her reply. She saw her mother smiling at the floor. She didn't want to be caught out again. She didn't want to offer him exactly what he expected.

'It's become my business because I'm the one who found him roaming the heath early in the morning, without any shoes, cold and frightened. You may think it a good idea but I don't. I don't think you realise what it's like on the heath. It's not an Arcadia, lovely as it is. The other day I intercepted some pervert trying to speak to Henry after you had just left him…'

'And so it's become your business to call the police, to inform on us, to watch us, carry my son around like a baby, make him hide things from me and generally treat him like an infant? You are entitled to ruin a public talk and to leave comments on my blog. I found *these*…' he paused for dramatic effect while he reached in his jacket pocket and pulled out the red plastic jellies. He dropped them with evident disdain on the coffee table. '…these disgusting plastic shoes'

They did look ugly on the table, all folded up from his pocket and slowly unfurling. The buckles showed traces of rust and caked earth clung to the soles. Anna wondered if he knew that to put shoes on a table was very bad luck. He continued.

'Do you expect a young boy to lie to his father to protect you? He has told me everything. I know all about the lady who likes to check up on him and whose mother lives opposite us. Apparently you pointed out your mother's house that first day when you called the police.'

'You lied to the police,' Anna took up the attack. 'You lied about having a stomach upset.'

Anna's mother uncrossed her legs and shifted in her seat. Henderson turned up the volume of his voice just a notch.

'Do you honestly believe that the police would understand the roaming child theory? Do you think that in this oppressive Western, consumerist society, with its overemphasis on the stifling Judaeo-Christian idea of a family unit and an absolute obsession with maternal influence, they would understand the necessity of teaching my child to survive and to learn freedom and independence?'

'Freedom? What does he have to be free from? "

'Freedom from the need for others,' he said, more quietly.

'I think *others* would think it pretty weird that you insist that your child walks home on his own at such a young age and without shoes. Surely, Mum, even you can see that's a bit wacko? And sorry, but don't we need others? Isn't that the whole point? That we do need others?'

Her mother remained silent, though perhaps her shoulders rose in a slight shrugging gesture. Her mother was predictably disappointing.

The light in the room changed as a cloud crossed the pink evening sun. Anna longed to get up and move around but she thought better of it. Her bones were pushing through her buttocks. She told herself that she had to endure it, that her discomfort would keep her alert and focused so that she wouldn't fall into any more of his traps.

'Your mother has told me something about you as a child.' His slippery velvety tone had returned.

Her mother raised her face and looked at her defiantly, her chin jutting out a little.

'Oh? And what sort of child was I?'

'By all accounts you were a frightened child. You mother recalls an incident when you followed her down the street in your nightclothes because you didn't want her to go out. Do you remember that?'

Anna had a vague memory of that evening, one of many distressing nights that she had tried to erase from her memory.

'Did my mother tell you that she used to leave me home alone from a very early age? The reason I was probably following her down the street was that I was hungry because she hadn't remembered to leave me anything to eat.'

'How ridiculous!' Now that she had finally spoken, Anna's mother's voice was croaky from lack of use. She cleared her throat. 'Are you really suggesting that I didn't feed you? Come on, Anna. You don't exactly look like a malnourished child. Ha ha.'

Anna thought she saw a trace of a smile on Henderson's face. She looked at the heavy fire poker and imagined slamming it down hard, first across her mother's head, then his.

'How would you describe yourself as a child? Let the adult self describe the child in you.'

'I admit that I was frightened a lot of the time. It is not a revelation to me and you are not helping me to have this revelation. I just need to make that clear. This house frightened me. It felt as if I was on my own in it too much because I was, in fact, on my own too much. I used to look out of the window of my bedroom and wish that I lived somewhere else with another family. The Goldblatts seemed to be having much more fun than me.'

'The Goldblatts? Jonathan and Ruth? What did you like so much about them?'

'They were a proper family. Jonathan was a great dad and Ruth a loving mother. The girls were that bit older than me but they always were so nice to me. I don't know why we are talking about them.'

'You brought it up.'

'Only to explain that I often wished I lived somewhere else. I could see into the Goldblatts' lives and they seemed so normal compared with mine. They had pets and board games and fun on Friday nights. I wanted to be with them.'

Her mother looked uncomfortable as she shifted in her chair.

'Even when your mother was here?'

Anna thought.

'Sometimes I think I felt alone and frightened even when Mum was here. I think she was a confusing parent. Sorry, Mum, but one minute you were loving, and the next you were snappy, and the next you were distant. I could never predict. It's not unusual, I suppose, for a drinker. I mean, I have friends with alcoholic parents or partners that describe much the same thing.'

Her mother stood up and burst into tears. Anna had witnessed this before. Many times. She watched, unmoved, as tears soaked her mother's cheeks. One left a small dark stain on her shirt, just above her left breast.

'Fine! So I'm a raging alcoholic who neglected and starved her child!'

Her mother stormed out of the room, banging her hip hard against one of the heavy chairs. They could hear her stomp downstairs. No doubt she went straight to the fridge and poured herself a glass of white wine. There was always an open bottle, ready and chilled, to help her through anything that she found a bit difficult.

Summer of Seven
The official blog of Professor Horace Henderson
BA (Yale), MS, PhD (Cornell)
July 3rd 2011

He looked across the space towards me and didn't smile. Finally he got himself onto the rope but he did not push himself off properly. He just swung out gently. I reached out as far as I could to try and grab his little body, but I could not. I was nowhere near within reach of him. The swing continued its pendulum, back and forth, with less and less conviction. Finally it came to a halt, leaving Uly hanging there, above the river bed. The drop below was about ten feet so I was not very worried. But then Uly looked at me. I saw that he was too exhausted to hold on for much longer. He shouted to me that he was getting too tired and that he was going to let go. Then he let the rope slip through his hands. It was like a slow motion movie. I shouted out his name. He fell and hit the river bed with a thud.

Comments: 34

Harrymetsally said:

I don't believe much in child-care experts and so came reluctantly to your lecture with my wife. However I was impressed by your attitude and it backed up some of the things I have been saying to my wife about her easing up on her anxiety that something terrible is going to happen to our kid. After your lecture we were at least able to have a discussion about my feelings. Thank you.

Pearlyteeth said:

This is without doubt one of the creepiest parenting blogs I have ever come across. You sound seriously deranged and it really concerns me not only that you work with children but that you have a child.

Buntycupcakes said:

I am taking your story as some sort of parable.

Takeitothebridge said:

This blog is a piece of crap. The only thing I agree with is that too many women are bunny boiling, stalking types.

Read more...

CHAPTER 17

'I'm keen to know something. Why have you befriended my mother?'

'I think she is an interesting woman.'

'Really?'

'Really.'

'You weren't using her as a means of getting to me?'

'No, though it is interesting that your style of parenting is the result of your determination to be totally different from your mother. It's a rather negative approach, don't you think?'

'But I had wonderful grandparents. I stayed with them in Somerset a hell of a lot. Maybe their loving ways with children rubbed off on me?'

'That's where your story of the hay barn came from, then?'

'Yes.'

She didn't care now.

'How many times have you watched Uly and me?'

'Sorry.?'

Henderson pushed his hair back from his face. His eyes swept down to the floor.

'How many times have you watched Henry and me?'

'I don't watch you. I only did that early on…'

'Why?' the Professor said.

'What?'

'Stalk us?'

'I believe Henry wanted and needed me. That's not exactly stalking, is it? Not when the "stalkee" has asked to be watched over.'

Anna caught a change of expression. Emotion felt and quickly hidden.

'Your mother says that you never knew your father?'

Another tactic to undermine her.

'I didn't. And judging by your blog your dad was a bit weird., wasn't he? '

'What's it like to be fatherless, Anna?'

'I only know what it is like to be without a father. I never felt the lack of him because he was never here. I said your dad was a bit weird wasn't he?'

'Did you never want to meet your father?'

'Yes, of course I did. The possibility that he might be more normal than my mother was appealing. I remember there were plans for me to meet him. But then he died. He was an artist, like my mother. They met at the Slade.'

'So you never met him?'

'No. And your father?'

'And you're sure this man was your father?'

She looked at him.

'What do you mean?'

'I think you had better talk to your mother because there may be a possibility of some uncertainty over this issue.' Anna's mind was racing. *Possibility of uncertainty over this issue?* Would her mother have expressed doubts to this man about her daughter's paternity? She did not want him to see that he had disturbed her.

'Yes. I will. It's between the two of us, don't you think? I mean, we barely know you.'

'Perhaps it is.'

Another pause while he looked steadily at her. Into her eyes. She tried not to flinch.

'Do you have a problem with fathers wanting an input into their children's lives, Anna?'

'Fathers are a concept I can appreciate, thanks. More than

appreciate, actually, since my own children have a father.'

'But I gather your husband's work left you to cope on your own rather a lot. You once said to your mother that you felt like a single parent but without any of the sympathy. Is that right?'

Her mother really had been talking – spilling the family beans. How many times had Henderson sat here before?

'Well, at the time it was a bit hard, but that's how we did it. David earned most of the money while I took care of the children and just worked a bit. Freelancing. A spot of writing for newspapers. I suppose it seems very traditional to you but it worked pretty well. I may have moaned a bit but I don't regret the time I spent with the children. Looking back, it was lovely. Really lovely. I admit that I'm very sad that it's over.'

She regretted the tight little smile she gave him.

'Do you think that your husband might have wanted to spend more time with the children?'

'Perhaps. I don't know. He hasn't said so.' She wasn't about to tell Henderson about David weeping in the tennis club.

Henderson sipped some water. She wanted some too. Her mouth was bone dry and tasted bitter.

'Was it you perhaps who prevented your husband from spending more time with the children?'

He was getting closer to her soft underbelly. She could not let him know.

'No, I don't think so.'

Henderson paused.

'How would you describe Henry?'

'I would describe him as a nervous, bright child. A bit frightened of everything.'

Henderson nodded.

'And on the first day you met him, was he frightened when you approached him in the park?'

Anna thought.

'No. He was very cold and his feet hurt but I wouldn't say that he was frightened. He was making an odd little noise as if to comfort himself. His burbling noise.'

Anna saw Henderson's nostrils twitch as he inhaled.

'Do you realise that you have described my son in the same way that you described yourself? As a frightened child?'

'Yes. Well, I believe that's true. It takes one to know one.'

She heard herself give a little bark of a laugh. Steady.

'Since the day you called the police, Henry has become more frightened. He is reluctant to do the activities and adventures I have set up for him on the heath. He has lost his innocence. He has lost his trust in me. And in himself. You do realise this is all because of you? That's what you have given him, Anna, and I'm angry about that. I'm very angry. I will have to take steps now to redress things.'

'I saw his face when you put him on that swing. Didn't you? Why did you force him to carry on when he obviously hated it? If you ask me, he'd be happier reading his dinosaur books at home.'

'I didn't ask you.'

In his face was revealed something close to hatred but once again he worked to restore his mask.

'A child needs to be tested. To find confidence in his own strength and resources.'

She worried that he was going to start talking about bloody Sparta again.

'Listen, Henderson. My children would have loved to go on that swing at that age. They were fearless. They were adventurous and confident. They still are. Do you think there is any possibility that it is because they felt protected by their parents and so with the knowledge of that protection behind them they were ready to zoom off into the unknown without a backward glance? What do you think of that? That they felt protected – not smothered or stifled, but protected?'

He smiled. He was not interested in her theories. He was the expert.

'Your mother tells me that you are rather overbearing with your children even now. She says that your daughter rarely comes back home and that you have only stayed one weekend with her. Is that right?'

Anna pushed away the sharp stab of pain.

'Don't take my mother's opinion too seriously.'

'But it's not just your mother. She has talked about your husband too...'

Anna held her breath. She felt winded. Don't bring David into this. Please don't. She exhaled, trying not to show that he had hit home.

'They're hardly great pals.'

'She says they had a talk recently because they were both worried about you.'

'I don't believe you.'

Henderson moved in his chair so that his jumbo cords were grazing the glass coffee table. He leaned further still, until she saw the glass cutting a horizontal line in the plump verticals stripes of his trousers.

'You see, Anna, I was thinking of calling the police. They might be more interested in you than me. Your mother and your husband would back me in saying you are stalking my son. As I said, they are very worried about your behaviour.'

'What?' Anna cried. 'What are they worried about? I'm not guilty of anything. Call the police! I'll tell them all about the swimming and the swing and the poky little woven cage on the heath that you make Henry stay in because of some weird stuff that went on in your childhood. I'm proud of the fact that I have stuck by him. That I didn't do what everyone else does and mind my own business. Isn't that what people always say when something terrible happens to a child? *Well, we knew that there was something going on but we didn't like to interfere.* Either that, or they feign absolute surprise. *But they seemed like the perfect family.'*

'Henry shouldn't have shown you the construction. That's nothing to do with you.'

'What you going to do? Punish him? For showing me the "nest"?'

Henderson pushed his hair away from his face and threw himself back in his chair, making it screech on the polished floorboards. His eyes were dark and glittery as he looked at her but still he was able to control his voice. Cold and even.

'Apparently, your husband has said that you are finding this a particularly difficult time. Your son is about to go to university and is away for a while this summer. I believe that you have also lost your job. Obviously you are finding things hard, particularly if you have been used to being overprotective as a mother.'

How dare he? Her real mortification came from hearing that David had spoken to her mother about her. He knew how she felt about her mother and she was furious that David had given Henderson the ammunition he needed against her. Because of David, Henderson had managed to hurt her.

'And then there was the loss of your third child.'

Anna froze.

'So. Taking all this into consideration... I'm not going to call the police,' Henderson said.

She could think of no answer. She had been betrayed by her mother and her husband, and he knew it.

Anna got up and ran out of the sitting room, down the stairs and into the street.

Summer of Seven
The official blog of Professor Horace Henderson
BA (Yale), MS, PhD (Cornell)
July 4th 2011

I ran, moaning like a wounded animal, calling out his name as my breath came in sharp bursts. I ran for what seemed like miles until I came to a small farm by a dirt road and ran straight in through the open swing door. An old farmer and his wife were sitting down to eat. The room smelled of dogs and boiled root vegetables. They put down their spoons when I began to talk and I remember feeling bad that they had only eaten half their soup. But someone had to drive me to my father. I just said that my brother was hurt and lying on the bottom of the dry river bed and would they please help me. I begged them to help me right there and then. I asked them to drive me to my father's house. We didn't have a phone because my father didn't think we needed one in the country.

Comments: 30

SarahK said:
What happened next? Is this a true story? Please tell us what happened.

Stargazer said:
You are freaking me out. If this is real then you need some help yourself and if you have just made this up then you still need help.

MissFunnypenny said:
WTF this blog is one of the maddest I've ever seen. I thought Horace Henderson was a well known child-care guru but to be honest this all seems desperately sad.

Muminthemiddle said:

My twelve year old son is always undermining me in front of his friends. This is the kind of behaviour he has watched his dad doling out to me on a daily basis. How can I get this to stop as it is really making me feel unhappy within my own home. Do you have any advice on this?

MrBojangles said:

I was really getting some intense enjoyment out of hearing about you manning up your son and all your rugged adventures. You are writing like a child now.

Read more…

CHAPTER 18

Through half-open eyes, Anna watched David getting ready to go to work. She hated the way his ankle bones clicked when he put on his socks. His violent drawing of the curtains irritated her, as did his disapproving little sniff as he left the room. In the bathroom next door, she heard him clear his throat into the sink. He brushed his teeth in his usual manic way and spat loudly.

He knew how she felt about her mother. If he was forming some sort of allegiance with her, he was in danger of completely destroying their marriage. Anna would not stay married to a man who plotted with her mother against her.

She lay in bed for hours, staring at the summer light burning through the heavy curtains, her eyes and head aching from her tangle of thoughts. She had heard her friends talk about being so low that they couldn't get out of bed but it had never happened to her before. She could smell the sourness of her own breath against the pillows, and when she touched her hair it was dull and dry. Her scalp felt itchy and squalid.

Defeated in her lone effort to watch over Henry, she now had no idea what to do. Should she go to the police and risk not being believed? Henderson as the authoritative, academic male would certainly hold sway over her, a mere mother.

She drifted in and out of half-sleep until the late afternoon, ignoring Winston, who jumped on the bed and whined and swiped her face with his large, crusty paw-pads. She yelled at him when he scratched her on the arm. He left the bedroom but continued to whimper though the crack in the door.

It was evening before she managed to get out of bed and make a cup of tea. She pulled on some jeans and a T-shirt and brushed her hair. She forced down a bowl of cereal, remembering how much she had disapproved when Jason had eaten cereal at any old time of day, pouring a quarter of the packet into a mixing bowl with half a pint of milk. The person she had been when her children had lived at home seemed to be entirely different to the one she was now.

A knock on the door made her panic. Winston was barking and hurling himself against it. She stood behind it and asked who it was. She heard a low voice.

'It's Alphonse. Please don't be angry that I have come round, Anna.'

God, that voice. Despite everything, her heart leapt with excitement. Winston growled.

'Please tell your dog that I just want to take you both out on the heath.'

She opened the door. Alphonse smiled at her. Once again, his attractiveness shocked her. Winston wagged his tail when Alphonse ruffled his head. She knew that she should feel irritated with him for coming round but she felt only delight.

'Moisette told me where you lived. I hope you don't mind. I have the afternoon off and wondered if you would come for a walk with me.'

Anna looked down at Winston, who looked up at her. He had heard the 'w' word.

'All right.' She reached out and grabbed her keys.

On the walk to the park, their bodies kept bumping together as Winston dragged her along. Each time, her response was visceral.

'How has work been?'

It was only a decoy. A way of pretending she was not physically drawn to him.

'Yesterday I went to a place called Baltham House. Have you heard of it?'

'No, sorry.'

'It is a place where mothers and children are forced to go while they wait to hear about their status as immigrants. It is a terrible place. Some of the children are very sick. They should not be in a place that is like a prison. I'm trying to help them, trying to sort out decent health provision for them. This place was meant to be so much better than the last but it is not.'

'I don't understand. Why are they there?'

'Oh, it's your government's way of hiding what is going on. They don't want British people getting upset when these immigrants are put on planes by private security firms at five in the morning. They are hiding them away from the public eye. But these people would not be in the UK unless something bad had happened to them. No one wants to leave their home, Anna. No one leaves their home unless they really have to.'

On the heath, the sun was shining through the trees.

'I'd rather not talk about it,' Alphonse said. 'I'm happier just to walk with you.'

She took him to a field at the top of the heath where the grasses were yellow and long. Alphonse walked right into the middle of it and disappeared. When she found him, he was lying on his back with his eyes open.

'If I do this then I can pretend that I am in the Congo. These grasses are like the grasses we have at home. When I was a boy and went hunting with my uncles I used to lie like this. The first time I went hunting, I dressed up in my smartest clothes. I wore a suit and tie and waited for them outside the compound. The men came, the villagers came, and they all laughed at me. They laughed so much that they couldn't stand up. It was the story of the year, I think. They made me undress and wear traditional clothes. They always called me Fred Astaire after that, because of that stupid suit.'

'Oh, really?' Anna was laughing.

'Although it's nice to look up at you with the sun behind you, you could come and lie down beside me. No one will see. No one will know we are here. We can talk. You can tell me about yourself.'

Anna did as he asked. She remembered his smell – like fresh soap. She liked looking at his face close up. She liked watching the soft movements of his mouth. Winston sniffed their heads.

'So what sort of things do you want to tell me? Do you have any secrets? The grasses won't tell.'

'Whispering grass.'

'What did you say?'

'Oh, there's this song.'

He laughed.

'How does it go?'

'Oh, no. I don't think I could…'

Anna started to sing, confident in her voice.

Why do you whisper, green grass?

Why tell the trees what ain't so?

'I can't remember the rest of the lyrics.'

He was silent for a bit.

'I like your voice. It's sweet. It's made me remember something I've not told anyone. Only one other person knows. It's quite bad so I hope you will still like me afterwards.'

Anna hoped it wasn't too bad. She didn't want to have to stop liking him.

'Sometimes I think about it and it makes me feel awful. My father had a car. A BMW. It was not that new, but it was still a BMW. A German car. Lots of people had little old, old VWs in the Congo, but only an important person would have a BMW. He put it into the shed where we kept the animal feed, and I don't know why, but one day I was in the shed with my friend Edwiche and we decided that it would be good to sit on top of the car and pretend that we were in a parade. We stood on the car and got a bit carried away and imagined all the girls looking up at us and we jumped on the car and even though we must have been about seven or eight and skinny, we dented the roof. We were so scared. We ran into the bush at the back of the house. When we came back, the housekeeper had been sacked and the son of our housekeeper had been beaten. They didn't believe him when he said that it wasn't him.'

'And you never confessed?'

'No, I never did.'

'Alphonse, that *is* bad. You must feel terrible about that. Sorry, but I can't tell you that is not bad.'

'I don't know what I should do about it. I sometimes feel I should go back and track down the housekeeper's son and apologise...'

He drifted off, lost in his own thoughts.

'I've probably got a secret as bad as that.'

He turned back to her, smiling. His face was close to hers.

'Yes, Anna. You have to tell me your secret now to make me feel better about mine.'

'Well, this is something I have never told anyone. I was pregnant with my third child. I was quite old – it must have been about eight years ago now. It wasn't planned.'

'Yes.'

She felt his arm pressing against hers. She was glad that he didn't try to do more.

'My husband wasn't happy about it. He was so angry with me for wanting the baby that he pushed me down the stairs. I hit my back very hard.'

'And you lost your baby?'

'Yes.' She felt her throat tighten. He knew and took her hand.

'I lost the baby at four months, and do you know what is really strange?'

'What?'

'We have never talked about it. David and me. We never talked about me going into hospital and having blood transfusions and the loss of the baby.'

The evening sun shone on the secret place they had created in a public park.

'Do you have any children, Alphonse?'

He turned to her.

'No, I was never blessed. I was married but no children came from it.'

'Tell me something.' Anna knew that she could confide in this man. 'If you had a seven-year-old child, would you let him walk home on his own, on the heath, early in the morning, barefoot and shivering with cold?'

'Certainly not. Why? Why are you asking me that?'

'It doesn't matter, but I'm really glad you said what you did. You gave the right answer.'

She let him kiss her and it seemed the simplest, most natural thing in the world when he lifted up her skirt, right there in the long grass, and put himself inside her. She felt his strength. She knew his sureness.

Later, back home, after they had parted with smiles of recognition, she was filled with joyful energy. She turned on the radio and danced in the kitchen, doing ballet leaps across the room, giggling to herself. Winston stared at her as if she were mad. Alphonse was her newest, truest and most beautiful friend. She was ashamed of nothing that had happened. It had been innocent. He had given her the courage to deal with everything. To try and fix everything in her life.

Summer of Seven
The official blog of Professor Horace Henderson
BA (Yale), MS, PhD (Cornell)
July 5th 2011

The farmer got up and steered my shaking, sobbing body towards his truck and drove the twenty minute journey to my house which was just outside Marystone Town with the water-tower set behind it. Father was sitting marking his students' work when we came in. I told him what had happened. It took a while for him to react. Then he took off his glasses. He asked me to slow down and repeat what I had just said. I told him one more time. He shouted right into my face. He said I should have known better than to go first across the river bed. If Uly had gone first, then I could have pushed him hard enough to get across. I remember feeling the farmer's arm go round my back as if he were trying to protect me against my father's blame. The farmer had to suggest to my father that surely they should be on their way, now, to the boy, to see if he could be helped. The farmer said that he would phone the doctor and get an ambulance to go down too. My father thanked him and explained where the swing was.

We drove as fast as we could. No one spoke. I couldn't even hear the sound of my father breathing. It was as if he was holding his breath until we reached the track that ran to the river bed. He drove so fast down that stony track that I was jerked out of my seat a dozen times. I split my eyebrow on the window. We parked the car and together we ran to the sycamore tree. We saw Uly lying there, looking up at us, his blood like a dark halo around his head. My father's scream sent the birds flying in fright. It was the ugliest sound I had ever heard. I wished I could fly away with them rather than watch as my father leaped into the air and down to my brother. When I did look down, my father was holding my brother's limp body in his arms. The ambulance men were soon there beside them. I saw them feel for Uly's pulse and shake their heads. Gently, they took Uly from my father and put his body on a stretcher with a blanket over his face. They passed him between them, upwards and out of the creek.

I wished so hard that it had been me who had died instead of my brother. For a moment, I considered throwing myself down into the ravine and hoping that my head would bang so hard against a rock that I would stop forever too. Or I could hang myself from the swing. Then my father would feel that justice had been done.

Father never spoke about that day. When the police interviewed me, I didn't tell them that it was part of a big adventure that my father had planned and that we were going to stay out all night. It was just a terrible accident, the kind of thing that happens when boys muck around near dry river beds. I never got a chance to tell my father that he could have saved Uly if he had taught him properly how to swing across that ravine. It was my father's fault that Uly had died swinging across the ravine.

Comments: 72

MoMa said:

I too had a distant, academic father who had strong ideas about how children should be raised (as a reaction to his own upbringing). I reacted against him by dropping out of school at fifteen. My own children are high-achievers, not as a result of me pushing them but because they don't want a similar chaotic struggle to mine. They want their lives to go in a straight line.

JackDGood said:

I know this is terrible but I experience feelings of real resentment towards my three year old son. There is no question that he comes first with my wife and when he comes into our bed in the morning he tells me: "Go away, Daddy!". More often than not I will get up and leave them there in bed together, all cosy and happy, and I sometimes feel like bursting into tears. What can I do about this?

SarahK said:

JackDGood, I don't think you will get a reply. Henderson has not responded to a single one of my comments. Self-important people who blog rarely do. I would say that your feelings towards your son are absolutely understandable. I seem to remember it was the same for my husband because my kids wanted to have me to themselves. Don't worry though because as they have grown up, they have needed their father in different ways. Although we are no longer together, there are some things they find easier to talk to him about.

SusanF said:

I am so desperately sorry for your loss. For such a thing to happen at such a young age and to be held responsible for it is truly terrible. I will pray for you.

Nancy said:

Where are you? Please contact me.

Read more...

CHAPTER 19

Anna decided that it was time to confront her mother. How dare she ambush her and force her to sit in a room with Henderson?

She drove angrily, parked, and was just crossing the road when she heard someone running and shouting after her. She turned and saw a woman with long limbs, wearing flappy, expensive linen. Henderson's wife.

'Excuse me!' she called. 'Could you just wait a moment? You're Sylvia's daughter, aren't you? I'm Nancy, Horace Henderson's wife.' She was squeezing between two parked cars to get to Anna, who had turned back. 'Look, I'll come straight to the point. I wonder if you know the phone number of the Goldblatts' cottage?'

Anna was cagey.

'No. I've been there, but about thirty years ago. Sorry, I've no idea.'

The woman's mouth trembled.

'I've tried phoning the Goldblatts at both our addresses back home but they don't seem to be there. I've tried Ruth's mobile but there's no response.'

'Oh dear.'

'And I've searched around for the details of the cottage but I can't find anything. Then I thought of your mother because she's such good friends with the Goldblatts but she says she doesn't have it. I was about to ask her again just in case she had suddenly remembered.'

Anna couldn't keep up the curt politeness.

'I'm sorry, but why are you asking me?'

Anna was surprised to see the woman's face redden.

'Look. I've come to a bit of a… dead end… and I hoped you might be able to help me find the phone number.'

'Has something happened?'

Nancy summoned up some control.

'It's just that my husband has taken my son down there and I'd like to join them as soon as I possibly can.'

Something had happened.

'When did they leave?'

'This morning. They left this morning after I'd gone to work. I'm fairly sure that they went to Hereford. That's the only other place in England that Horace knows. He went down a month ago, but on his own.'

'Right. So you think that they are there?'

Anna looked at Nancy, and from her open, anxious expression, guessed that she knew nothing about the feud between her husband and herself.

'Yes, I hope so. I really hope they are there.'

'Is everything all right?'

Nancy paused, as if she was working out what to say. Her smile was tight.

'He probably just forgot to leave me the address. Horace and Henry are having a very intense father/son bonding experience just now. Horace is concentrating on Henry so much that he forgets everything else.'

The woman gave a small, nervous laugh.

'If I get the address for you, how are you going to get there? You realise how far Herefordshire is from London, don't you? It's a five-hour drive away.'

'It's that far? I'll have to take a train. I haven't driven for years.'

'Look, I'll get the address from my mother. I'm sure she has it. I'll be right back.'

'Oh, thank you. Thanks so much.'

'Well, I haven't got it yet but I'll certainly try.'

Anna pressed the doorbell so hard that her fingernail grew white at the bent tip. Henderson's wife's anxiety meant this was not the time to have it out with her mother. That would have to be postponed.

Her mother opened the door. Her earth-covered hands and her baggy sixties smock told Anna she had been gardening. There was no smile for Anna. Her mouth was a flat line.

'Oh, hello? I hear that Horace has managed to get you to leave him and his boy alone. He said that you realised that your behaviour was completely unacceptable.' She gave a tight, satisfied little smile but her eyes were hard. 'Oh, and Natasha tells me that you were pretty upset that I had been to her cottage before you.' Her smile got wider. And more cruel.

Anna remembered Henry. The need to sort things out made her cold.

'Sorry, I haven't got time for any of this. I need the address of the Goldblatts' cottage. I believe Henderson's wife has already asked you for it.'

She felt a need to be absolutely straight and firm.

'I don't have it. I'm so sorry.' Her mother folded her arms like a petulant child. 'Come on, Anna. So you haven't learned your lesson after all. Keep your bloody nose out of that family's business.'

'You must have it. I don't know why you are protecting that horrible man. Even his wife seems worried now. I think that he has taken Henry off to Herefordshire without telling her.'

'I'm afraid I don't know his wife. He's the one who talks to me and says hello and good morning. I hardly ever see her. In fact, he seems to do all the parenting, if the truth be told, while she is away at her fancy job.'

'Look, Mum. I think that Henderson was only interested in you because it was a way of getting at me.'

Her mother started to laugh a dry, barking laugh. Devoid of humour. Anna had to step back to get away from her spite.

'You just can't bear it if someone actually likes me, can you?'

Anna so wanted to give her mother a good hard push. She clenched her hands behind her back.

As the tired and hurtful refrain began again, Anna caught sight of a familiar book. It was green leather embossed with gold and it glinted in the evening light. The book seemed to be on her side. Anna pushed past her mother and grabbed it, placing her index finger on the small square 'G' and flipping it open. There it was. The third address down – 'Goldblatts' Cottage'. Ignoring her mother's shouts of protest, Anna seized the book and walked out.

When Nancy opened the door, Anna's heart was beating fast.

'I've got it.'

The woman breathed a long sigh of relief, held out her hand for the book, and tapped out the number on her mobile. Anna noticed a blue vein pulsing in her temple. Nancy let it ring… and ring… then snapped it shut.

'No answer.'

'What happens when you try his mobile?'

'Oh, Horace doesn't believe in mobiles. He thinks that they affect brain patterns. I never use mine when he's around.' She blinked, a blink almost as heavy as her son's. 'OK. I've got the address. All I need to do is get to Paddington.'

She seemed to be talking to herself more than to Anna, gathering her thoughts.

'I mean, Horace went to Hereford before and I know he planned to take Henry over the summer. So that must be it. He decided to take him and forgot to tell me.'

'I'll drive you to the station. Come on. Grab what you need. I'll wait for you in the car.'

Nancy stared at Anna in amazement.

'It makes sense. My car is right here. Come on.' She heard herself give a little laugh.

'Well, if you're sure.'

'Yes. I'm sure.'

Anna got the road atlas out of the boot and looked up the small village of Langston at the foot of the Black Mountains. She leaned the battered map against the wheel of the car. Nancy sat in the passenger seat, her back straight, a big leather bucket bag on her lap.

Anna turned to her. 'Look, I have a suggestion. I'm pretty sure that the cottage is in the middle of nowhere. I've looked it up on the map and it would be almost impossible for you to get to it by train. If you are really worried about your son, then I'll drive you there.'

Nancy looked at her. 'Why would you do that?'

'Because I know what it is like to be desperately worried about one's child.'

'Thank you,' Nancy replied, relief overcoming her initial protests. 'That is amazingly kind of you. I was just thinking what I would do if I arrived as night was falling, in the middle of the countryside, and I've never even been to Wales.'

Anna decided not to enlighten Nancy about Herefordshire not being in Wales.

'Well, don't worry. Let's just get going, shall we? Before it gets too dark.'

CHAPTER 20

Having thought through the route, Anna set off towards the M4. She would head for the Severn Bridge to Wales and then on to the border. Nancy put her neat head back on the headrest. When Anna glanced at her, she saw that she had closed her eyes. Was she going to sleep? Her apparent calm made Anna want to talk, to confess to her how concerned she had been about Henry. She cleared her throat loudly and Nancy opened her eyes. She had not been asleep.

'I need to tell you that I am more involved with your son and husband than I admitted.'

Nancy turned to her.

'What do you mean?'

'Well, I have met Henry and your husband before. On the heath and round about.'

Anna waited for her shocked response.

'OK. I'm going to come clean too,' Nancy said. 'I do know about you because Horace has told me about you. At first I believed him when he said you were a mother having a nervous breakdown because your children had left home. Then I read his blog and realised how confused he is himself. When I saw you crossing the road just now, I thought that you were probably the only person who could help me. I've been trying to think of a polite way of telling you that you are known in our family as "The Doorstep Woman".'

Nancy started to cry. It took Anna by surprise after her rational account. Soon she was sobbing uncontrollably. Anna felt for the tissues in her side pocket and offered them. 'Tell me what you think is going to happen, Nancy. Tell me, please?'

Nancy's head was turned towards her.

'First tell me what you know about Henry and Horace.'

'I found him on his own on the heath. He was shivering and barefoot and all alone and I took him home. Your husband didn't thank me; in fact he was rude. He said he wanted him to walk home alone.'

Anna looked at Nancy, who nodded to tell her to continue.

'I started going to the pond where your husband went swimming on Sundays. Then when the summer holidays started, I went every morning just to make sure that Henry was OK. I made sure that your husband didn't see me.'

'I don't understand. You hid until my husband left?'

'Yes. You do know, don't you, that he always left Henry to walk home across the heath on his own?'

'Yes, I am aware of that.'

'Well, anyway. Henry seemed to want me to be there.'

'How do you know that?'

Anna heard a flash of defensiveness in Nancy's voice.

'Oh, because he asked me. He seemed reassured that I was there.'

'Oh, is that right?' Nancy said tightly.

'Later, Henry showed me the swing. Did you know about the swing?'

'Yes, yes I know about it.'

Anna thought that Nancy spoke a little too fast. Was it possible that she knew less than she was letting on? 'Well… then it got more complicated. My mother, who worships your husband, set up a meeting and ambushed me into meeting him. That was when he confronted me about my watching over Henry.'

She thought she felt Nancy bristle.

'Your husband warned me off. He told me that he would call the police just as I had called the police on you.'

'You were the one who called the police on us?'

'Yes.'

Nancy blew her nose again and enquired about Anna's own children. The sound of tears had gone from her voice. Anna told her about Natasha and Jason.

When Nancy finally spoke again, she had regained her composure. Her voice was clear and strong.

'When we came to England, things just seemed to come together. You know that Horace's father was the highly respected classicist, Benjamin F. Henderson?'

Anna shrugged her shoulders. She had never heard of him.

'Some of Horace's ideas have a Hellenic slant because of the paternal influence. He believes that a healthy boy should start to move away from his mother at the age of seven. Current child studies and a lot of Horace's work consistently back that up. So it was fortuitous that Henry hit seven pretty much as we arrived in London. I should add that back home, Horace had run into a bit of trouble. A boy he was working with ran away and went missing. He was found, safe and well, but some of Horace's less successful colleagues at the institute took advantage of the event and used it against him.'

Anna nodded. She knew all this already.

'Horace insisted that we live by the heath. It is an ideal place for creating adventures for Henry... adventures that would teach him self-reliance and a love of nature. He had read about the heath in the States... about it being something of a paradise. Horace was already committed to writing a paper about the impact of nature and adventure on a seven-year-old boy. The blog was to be a sort of practice run.'

'And you, Henry's mother, are supposed to just let him go. Hand him over? Is that what you agreed to do?'

Nancy sighed. 'Well, the other important reason we came to London is that I am working at the Felderston Centre, in the Adolescent Mental Health Unit. It's a great job. It's the kind of thing

I always dreamed of back in the States. I can't tell you what a great opportunity it was for me. I have to start pre-school sessions really early and I'm often back late so I am not there for Henry very much.'

So she was a child psychologist too. Poor Henry. Anna tried to concentrate on her driving but the discussion fascinated her.

'I do agree that mothers don't trust fathers enough to play a part in their children's lives,' Nancy continued. 'Fathers are made to feel redundant and untrustworthy so it's no wonder that they behave in disappointing, irresponsible ways.'

Anna felt increasingly impatient. What about Henry? Why wasn't Nancy talking about Henry?

'Sorry, but I have heard all this from your husband,' she interrupted. 'And I've read his muddled blog about Greece and Sparta and the age of seven. What I really want to know is if you think Henry is in any danger from your husband's ideas and practices. What do you think?'

Nancy said nothing. When Anna turned to look at her, she saw that her lips were pursed. Anna waited. The silence continued. Anna put her foot down. Maybe it was an act of pure frustration. She moved into the fast lane to overtake a lorry, the headlights from the cars on the other side of the motorway and the blur of backlights on their side flashing past them.

Nancy clutched the dashboard. 'You're driving too fast. You're frightening me.'

'I want to know what's going on. You must tell me. Do you understand?' Anna still had her foot down on the accelerator. 'I won't slow down until you talk to me.'

'OK... but slow down... please believe me when I say I never thought Horace would go this far. Of course I didn't. You have to believe me. Please slow down.'

Anna let her foot off the accelerator. Just a little. She was still driving at more than a hundred miles an hour. The Volkswagen's engine sounded strained and it had started to judder.

'You think Horace is going to force Henry to endure some even more outrageous challenge, don't you? You think that your loony husband is going to leave your seven-year-old son out all night on the fucking mountains. Expose him to the elements just to prove something. Oh my God! Poor Henry! Why didn't you protect him?'

She could feel her own spit hitting her hands as she drove. All the pent-up rage she felt towards Henderson, her mother, David and her work was spilling out over the women who sat next to her. She wanted to frighten her, as she had been frightened by Henderson's idiocy.

'Let's call the police, the mountain rescue team, the bloody army!' Anna shouted.

'Please slow down, Anna,' Nancy said. Anna moved into the middle lane and went down to eighty miles an hour. The engine was still juddering.

'Well? Why aren't you phoning the army? I told you I want you to phone the bloody army.'

Nancy spoke quietly. 'I think we should wait until we get there. I'm hoping they haven't set off yet. We really can't summon a search team until we know exactly what is going on. We can't send people off into the mountains at night until we are quite certain that my husband and Henry are out there.'

Anna was crying now. She should have called the police straight after her meeting with Henderson at her mother's. She shouldn't have given Henderson a chance to make his next insane move.

'Henry is scared of his father. That was why he wanted me there. Didn't you notice that Henry didn't want to be alone with his father? It doesn't take a professional to see that. And this accident involving your husband's brother? I read about it in the blog.'

Nancy was sitting bolt upright now. She trembled as she spoke. 'I know, I know. I didn't read the blog properly until this morning.

I helped Horace set it up because I thought it would help him achieve what he wanted with his sabbatical. I was shocked by what it revealed about his state of mind. I didn't link his training of Henry with his brother's accident. He never told me the details. But I do want to say that before you got involved and called the police, Henry didn't seem nervous of his father. He went off with him very enthusiastically.'

'Or was that the image he showed you? To please you... because you were part of the team. The whole experiment. Perhaps I was the only person he could talk to?'

'Can you really judge me, Anna? Can you really be so confident about your own mothering? Are you sure that you have got it right? How do your children feel about you?' Nancy's voice was strong and more confident.

'No, of course I'm not bloody sure I got it right as a mother. At the moment I am a bit surplus to requirements... But they are grown up... nearly.'

'And do you think the growing distance from your own children made you want to watch over my son?'

'No, I don't. I was behaving as a citizen, not a mother. It would have been very easy for me to walk away, wouldn't it? As everyone seems to have wanted. But maybe there would be fewer missing, hurt and dead children if we didn't look the other way.'

Nancy didn't say anything. Anna could hear her heavy breathing. 'Is it conceivable, Anna, that your spying on my husband is the reason why he fled to the mountains?'

Anna groaned.

'It might make you feel better to blame me rather than yourself for taking your eye off the ball, but Henry was already talking about a big adventure – a serious trial – some time ago, soon after I met him.'

Anna felt desperately tired and when she blinked, her eyes burnt. She wanted to rest her head somewhere. To lean it against the driving wheel. She was not sure. She was not sure about anything.

'I don't think you can blame me for this, Nancy... I really don't think I made any of this happen. It was your responsibility to stop him going on the swing. It was your responsibility to make sure a little boy did not sit like an animal in that woven cage in a wood...'

'The what?'

'The cage. You don't know about the cage?'

Nancy turned, her mouth slightly open.

'No, I didn't know about the cage.'

Anna heard fear.

'Henderson made a cage for Henry to sit in. He called it a nest but it was a horrible, pokey cage. Henry had to sit in it every day before coming home. Henderson left fruit in it. I suppose he thought he was keeping him outdoors and free but he was controlling him. He inflicted this on his son.'

Nancy's head was in her hands.

They were approaching the Severn toll bridge. As they drove across, light flashed on the expanses of clay mud. Nancy was crying. Anna's phone began to beep. David. She had not told him where she had gone. He could wait. On the smaller roads, Nancy craned her neck forward, peering into the darkness. Anna pulled over and turned on the overhead light to look at the map. Nancy leant over.

'Let me help, Anna. I'm good at maps. I can do the map reading.'

Nancy put her finger on the page and traced the roads.

'Look, there should be a crossroads coming up. We turn right, and then it should be straight into Langston. It shouldn't be too hard to find.'

Anna drove and Nancy called out directions. Soon they saw a sign to Langston. The road started to ascend, to twist and turn. An owl flew in front of the car, illuminated by the full beam of the headlamps. Nancy, already nervous, put her hand up to her chest and gasped. Then, round another bend, they saw the village sign post. They read it out loud in unison.

Anna had no idea where Julip Cottage was. She tried to remember but in the dark she could recognise nothing. It had been too long.

They drove slowly through the long village, looking for someone to ask instead of having to drive back and forth, up and down the main road, hoping for a clue. Anna noticed that one of the houses close to the road was lit up, and parked the car on the verge. Using her mobile as a torch, she walked up the garden path and knocked on the door. She heard movement and voices inside the cottage. A woman's voice called out. Anna told the voice that she was looking for Julip Cottage. She thought she sounded stilted and odd in the dark night and she worried she had woken every soul in the village. An elderly woman opened the door. A television blared in the background.

'I'm so sorry to disturb you. I know it's very late but could you possibly tell me where to find Julip Cottage?'

'Who wants to know?' She wasn't as friendly as she looked. Anna felt a wave of panic. She felt tears pricking in her eyes.

'Well… do you know the Goldblatts?'

'No. I don't know no one of that name.'

'Well, I think they have owned Julip Cottage for the last twenty or thirty years.' Anna tried not to sound exasperated.

'The Golds? You mean the Golds. We call them the Golds.'

'Well, the Golds then. We're friends of theirs from London. I've known Jonathan and Ruth for years. And the girls. Rebecca and Sara.'

'More like women now.'

The old woman looked at her suspiciously. Obviously Anna was not such a close friend as she made out.

'Could you give me directions to the cottage? I've come to see some friends staying there.'

'My husband was out walking the dog past Julip this evening. Up towards the sloping meadow. He saw a man and a boy in the garden there.'

Anna wanted to whoop with joy. They were there. It had to be them. A man and a boy. They were close. Close on their trail.

'Yes. Could you possibly tell me how to get there?' She pointed towards the car.

'There's a small turning, first left. Take that and you will see a farm on your right. Don't stop there but carry on and then you will see a track on the right. That leads to Julip Cottage. There's a sign by the roadside if you look out for it.'

'Thanks. Thank you. So, left and past the farm and then a track on the right.'

'That's it. It's not difficult. Goodnight.'

'Goodnight. Goodnight and thank you. Sorry for disturbing you.'

The woman suddenly smiled. 'I was watching a Cary Grant film. I'm mad about Cary Grant, me. My hubby's in bed and I'm up to watching Cary on me own.' She giggled like a naughty child.

'Yes... anyway, thanks so much.'

Anna waited until the woman had closed the door and then ran down the path and jumped into the driving seat. She turned to Nancy.

'She said her husband saw a man and boy at the cottage. It has to be them, doesn't it?'

Nancy started to shake. 'Take me there, Anna. Quickly. Let's go.'

Anna felt a jolt of recognition as the headlights hit the purple, slate-brick walls of the cottage. She remembered how the stone pieces seemed magically balanced on top of one other, without any visible bonding. She could recall something of coming here with Rebecca and Sara, and their parents and her mother. She remembered the steep hillside that rose up behind the cottage. She tried not to think that perhaps there was no one there after all.

She left the headlights on. Both women got out of the car at the same time. They ran and stumbled towards the door. Anna's hand hesitated for a moment before she pulled back the heavy knocker and let it bang hard. Twice. The women waited. Anna knocked twice again, even louder. The sound was magnified by the darkness and filled the garden around them. Again there was silence. Nancy pushed Anna aside and started knocking. She banged furiously six or seven times, an urgent, desperate noise. She shouted the names of her husband and her child, yelling up towards the windows.

'Perhaps they are asleep and can't hear us,' she said, sheer desperation in her voice. 'I mean, that sometimes happens, doesn't it? Horace! Henry!'

Anna thought she heard something behind her and turned. If there was movement, it was caught by the wind and blown away. She stared into the blackness but could see nothing but the faint outline of trees at the end of the garden. She took Nancy by the arm and led her back to the car. Nancy seemed to be in shock.

CHAPTER 21

For a few moments, they sat in silence in the car. Anna rested her head on the wheel.

'I think we should break in,' Anna whispered.

'How?' Nancy said.

'I'm sure we'll find a way.'

Using the small, concentrated light from Anna's mobile, they climbed out of the car and walked right round the house. Nancy stumbled and took Anna's arm. Anna felt the other woman's anxiety – the trembling of her body and her rapid heartbeat. They tried each ground-floor window but they were firmly locked. Returning to the car, they perched on the warm bonnet and stared up. Anna noticed that the small window just above the porch was slightly open. Below it was a large water butt pushed into the corner where the porch wall met the wall of the house. A pipe ran into it from the guttering. She ran towards it, the car's headlamps giving her sufficient light. She managed to pull herself on to the water butt, its hard plastic ridges cutting into her knees. Her hands reached for gaps in the stone walls, which she used to lever herself up. Finally she was upright and balanced on the edge. She tried to think of herself as light and feline. Stretching up, she got her feet on to the roof of the porch and then the rest of her body, until she was lying flat. She felt along the sharp tiles and crawled inch by inch until she was right up against the wall of the house. Slowly, steadily, she stood up. The windowsill was at chest height. She pushed as hard as she could to force open the window. Her heart leapt when it gave, and she was able to pull herself up and slither inside. She fell on to a cold floor. She was in the bathroom. For a few seconds she lay there registering the familiar smell of coal tar soap and the sound of a dripping, old-fashioned toilet cistern.

'Anna!' Nancy's desperate voice called from below.

'I'm in,' Anna shouted. 'I'll come down and open the door. Hang on.'

She suddenly felt the weight of darkness from the bathroom pressing behind her. She turned quickly and bravely into it, although she felt the fear would paralyse her if she let it take hold. She turned on the light of her phone and held her hands in front of her until they touched a wall and brushed against a light cord. She pulled it, half expecting to be confronted by the blinking sweetness of Henry or the looming Henderson. Instead, the light from the bathroom threw its glow into a small hallway, where Anna saw a light switch. She remembered this house, with its low ceilings, white walls and conker-coloured, sloping wooden floors. She went down a small flight of stairs and through another room to the entrance hall. Nancy burst in, squinting at the bright lights.

'Have they been here?'

'I haven't had a chance to look yet.'

Hand in hand, they ran into the kitchen. There was a pile of dinosaur books by a milky cereal bowl on the table. Nancy fell upon them.

'Henry's books!'

'Come on. Maybe they are upstairs.'

They went back up the stairs, Nancy clutching one of Henry's dinosaur books in her hand. Outside the first room they both hesitated before pushing open the door. It was a small bedroom with rush matting on the floor and a single unmade bed. The crumpled tartan rug suggested that Henry had been there.

They moved into the other bedroom. A double bed, unmade. A denim shirt flung on top of the chest of drawers. A pair of khaki shorts on the floor. Then both women were running downstairs. Outside, Nancy screamed the names of her husband and child. Then she was walking fast into the night, still shouting, but the only reply was the sound of the breeze from the mountain rustling the trees in the garden. Anna knew that she had to remain calm and to make decisions for both of them. She had read about this. It was called the golden hour – the time just after someone went missing when the police had the biggest chance of tracking them down. Perhaps the golden hour was long over. She went up to Nancy and touched her arm.

'Look, we can't just go walking about out there, searching on our own. We can't go on the mountains in the dark. We have no idea where they are. We have to tell the police and the rescue services. Tell them that we think a small child is out on the mountain alone. They know the terrain. They'll help us. Quickly.'

Nancy was frozen. Rooted to the spot. Anna ran into the house and found the phone on a table. She rang 999. A male voice answered. Anna's own voice was crisp with anxiety. 'Hello. Yes. We have just driven down from London and were expecting to meet up with a man and a boy who are staying at a cottage in Langston. We have reason to believe that they are lost on the Black Mountains somewhere.'

'Do you consider this to be an emergency?'

'Yes. Definitely. The boy is only seven and we don't know if he is with his father. We think that they might have become separated.'

She heard Nancy come in through the open front door. She stood beside her as she spoke. Anna saw that Nancy's smart linen trousers had black earth at the knees.

'You say that you have arrived at a cottage, having set off from London, and your friends are not there when you expected them to be?'

'Yes.'

'Did they know you were coming down?'

'Well, no. No, they didn't know.'

'Have you tried phoning their mobiles?'

'The man doesn't own a mobile. He doesn't believe in mobiles.'

Nancy moved forward and held out her hand for the phone. Anna pushed down a feeling of irritation.

'Hello… I am the man's wife. I believe he is having some sort of nervous breakdown or psychotic episode. I am a psychologist. I have been concerned for a while. I am also pretty sure that he has left my child out on the mountains. From something he said to me earlier. Please come quickly. My child is probably alone and in danger… wait a moment, please…'

She asked Anna for the address and directions to the cottage, then relayed them calmly to the operator. She put down the receiver.

'The mountain rescue team and the police will be here in twenty minutes.'

Twenty minutes was a long time.

CHAPTER 22

The light on the old-fashioned answer machine was flashing. Anna pressed Play. The voice was her mother's.

'Horace, I thought I'd better warn you that my daughter and your wife are on their way down. My daughter managed to grab the address book and knows where the cottage is. The two of them are driving to Hereford right now. At least that's what I presume. Anyway, I thought you might be interested. I'm not sure what's going on. Anyway, bye for now. Hope everything's OK. It's Sylvia, by the way.'

Anna shook her head and looked at Nancy.

'I'm not sure if your husband will have heard this or not. I can't remember how these old answer machines work. Would the light continue to flash?'

Nancy sat on the sofa. She looked exhausted. She did not reply.

'I'm worried he might have taken Henry somewhere else because he heard from my mother that we were on our way,' Anna tried again.

Nancy sighed.

'I don't know. I just don't know. I really don't know anything anymore, Anna. Let's just wait for the rescue team.'

Nancy scrabbled in her bag and brought out a packet of cigarettes. She lit up and drew in the first smoke, narrowing her eyes. Her hands were shaking.

Anna had not had smoked for years but she took a cigarette from Nancy and lit it. The dry bitter taste of the tobacco matched her mood exactly, but it also made her retch. She stubbed it out. Wanting to get rid of the ashy taste in her mouth, and feeling desperately hungry, she searched the kitchen and found some apples, still wrapped in cling film from the motorway service station. Evidence of a picnic meal snatched by Henderson and Henry on their way down. She filled two glasses with water and offered them, with the apples, to Nancy, who simply shook her head. Did she even see what Anna offered?

Time passed excruciatingly slowly. Anna paced the room. Nancy sat in shock.

'Do you think we should start looking?' Anna asked.

'No. We must wait for the emergency team. It won't help Henry if we get lost too.'

Five minutes later, Nancy asked Anna the same question and it was Anna's turn to advise on the side of caution.

Anna turned off the overhead light and slumped in a large armchair next to the sofa. There was enough light from the lamp next to the telephone. When she leant her head back and closed her eyes, she saw Henry's face. Henry's eyes. *Blink, blink.* Was Nancy imagining her son's face? Or Henderson's?

'Horace was very impressive, you know,' Nancy said after a long silence. 'I had never met anyone like him – the way he spoke to his students and the care with which he taught us. I think I fell in love with him the first time I walked into the lecture hall and saw the tallest man I had ever seen. But Horace is so moral, so absolutely correct. There was no question of us getting together until I had graduated. None at all. He can get very passionate about things, you know. He is a very passionate man.'

Anna did not answer. She got up and walked out of the room. She was alert to every sound that whispered in the darkness outside. A rustle of wind in the branches or the call of a bird made her jump. The darkness seemed deeper and more impenetrable then when they had been outside themselves, trying to open the windows. Then she remembered that she had not returned David's phone call.

'Hello. David, it's me.'

'Where the hell have you been?'

'I'm in Hereford.'

'Hereford?'

'Yes.'

She held receiver away from her ear as his anger exploded.

'I've been climbing the walls here. Why didn't you at least leave a note to tell me where you were? I was about to phone the police. I was lying in our bed wondering if you had left me or been killed. I'd decided I would rather you had been killed. It's four in the morning, Anna, and you're in Hereford! What? Did you just fancy a trip? Have you completely lost the plot?'

'Henderson told me that you had been talking to my mother about me. How could you do that? You must know how I would feel about that.'

'I thought we'd settled all the Henderson shit before we went to see Nat. I didn't know what to do. Your mother phoned me up and told me that it was still going on, which I suspected anyway because you started getting up at the crack of dawn again almost as soon as we got back. Your mother said that this professor was accusing you of taking an unhealthy interest in his child. I don't think your interest is unhealthy but God knows you do have an interest and I thought it was because you were missing the children so much, so that's what I told her. That's all I told her. I had to give her some reply. What else could I do?'

'So she phoned you. Not the other way round.'

'Yes, Anna, she phoned me. Now tell me why you are in Hereford at four in the fucking morning. Have you left me?'

Anna got up and looked out of the window. She was distracted by Nancy walking across the garden through the stream of light that fell from the open front door.

'Anna? Are you still there?'

'I'm here because Henderson's wife needed me to drive her down here.'

'What? She asked you to drive her?'

'No. I offered.'

David exhaled. A low groan of despair.

'Why did you do that? Why would you do that and not tell me? Don't you understand how your behaviour affects other people?'

'Look, David, that's not how it happened. It's complicated but, believe me, what I suspected is real. It's not just me imagining things this time. His wife is frightened too. Absolutely terrified.'

'So what are the two of you doing now?'

Nancy had disappeared. What on earth was she doing out there in the darkness?

'We're waiting for the rescue team and police to come. I should have ignored all of you and kidnapped him or something. I shouldn't have cared what any of you thought.'

'You're sounding crazy, Anna. You think you should have kidnapped him?' David sounded more exhausted than exasperated.

'David, I'm sorry if I've frightened you. I wasn't thinking. There didn't seem to be time to think about anything or anybody else.'

David didn't say anything. She could hear him breathing.

You told my mother about the baby but not how it happened.

'OK, Anna. Let me make sure I have this straight. You and Henderson's wife are there in the cottage having called the police and rescue services?'

'Well, actually, I'm not sure about Nancy. She went into the garden just now. I'm looking out into the garden and I can't see her…'

Anna's voice trailed off. Where was she?

'Look, I'd better go, David.'

We can never talk about it. But I cannot be with you because you killed our baby. I've had sex with someone who is kind and good. Kindness is such a rare quality.

'Don't hang up, Anna. At least while I've got you on the phone, I know you're OK.'

'Don't worry. The rescue services will be here soon. I'll ring you and tell you what's happening. I promise. Don't worry. Get some sleep before work. I'll be fine.'

'I'd drive down right now to be with you. You know that, don't you, Anna?'

'If I hadn't taken the car.'

Not saying Goodbye, she was already moving towards the front door. She called out to Nancy as she stepped into the night. It was then that she saw them, bearing down on her like ghosts. A huge man, made ghoulish by the light from the hallway, and Nancy with her filthy linen trousers flapping like sails. They walked grimly towards her.

CHAPTER 23

Anna stepped backwards. She turned and ran into the downstairs toilet, shut the door and pulled across the small bolt. She reached into her pocket, hoping she would feel the slim, reassuring shape of her mobile, but it wasn't there. She must have left it on the table. She could hear them right outside the door. The handle began to turn.

'Anna, come on out,' Nancy said.

Anna sat on the closed toilet seat, head bowed, with her hands between her legs. Was it all a plan? Had she been enticed here deliberately so they could get rid of her once and for all? Then they could do what they liked to their son. She looked up at the photo of the perfect Goldblatts in ski gear on a mountain top, all of them standing smiling in height order. Anna had never been skiing.

'Come out of there, Anna. Horace promises he will explain to me what's going on and where Henry is, but he wants you out of the house first.'

Anna stood on the loo and tried to push open the window. It was locked and anyway Anna knew it was too small to get her body through. And what would she do if she did manage to get out of the house?

'Please come out, Anna. Don't you understand! Horace says that he will only talk to me once you have gone,' Nancy said. Her voice was shrill.

Anna didn't believe a word of it. She didn't trust anything Henderson said – to her or to his wife. Maybe Nancy was deceiving herself.

There was a loud bang against the door. She imagined Henderson's massive hands punching it.

'I'm going to smash the door down unless you come out of there.' It sounded as if his face was pressed right up against the door, as if he wanted his voice to reach her close up. She stood up. Then there was a terrible pause.

'I warned you. I did warn you.'

And then it came. A terrific thud somewhere near the middle of the door. It sounded like he had taken a running kick at it. Anna shook as she cowered in the furthest corner. She heard Nancy shouting 'No!' and then another almighty kick, cracking the wood just by the door's hinge. Next time he would smash through one of the panels or bust the lock. She waited, her head tucked in her lap, tears running down her face. But nothing happened. She heard their voices moving away from her, and then more voices. Male voices. Calling out.

It had to be the rescue team. If it was the rescue team, she could let herself out. She had to pull hard on the battered door hard before it would open, then walked down the hallway. There were four men in orange waterproof jackets with loops of rope hanging off their belts, all standing in the hall with grim, just-woken faces. They all looked at her. A youngish man spoke first. His voice was gruff and matter-of-fact. He wiped his nose with the back of his hand.

'The police have informed us that a father and son are on the mountains and that the child has become separated from his father? Who is the mother here, please?'

'I am.' Nancy stepped out from the kitchen. She looked nervously at Anna. Where was Henderson?

'We were told that a dad has gone with his kiddy on the mountains,' the man repeated.

'My husband… Henry's father… was here just a moment ago. He ran off when he saw you coming. I was trying to get him to tell me where my son was.'

'And he was about to attack me,' Anna said, looking at Nancy. 'He would have hurt me if these men hadn't turned up…'

'He saw you through the front window, Anna. Please believe me when I say he said that he wouldn't talk to me while you were in the house. I was going to ask you to sit in the car or something, just so he would tell me where Henry was, but you locked yourself away.'

The young man spoke impatiently.

'Can we get the facts straight here, please? The father was here a minute ago? But we were told he was out on the mountain.'

An older man with a handsome, craggy face stepped in. 'All right, Trevor. That's enough.' He turned to Nancy and Anna. 'Can you explain? We were told that the father and son were out on the mountain. Now you are saying that the child is definitely alone.'

'Look, my husband is unwell. He is not himself. When we phoned, he wasn't here. Then he came back and I was desperately trying to get him to tell me where he had taken my son, but he wouldn't speak while Anna was in the house. He and Anna dislike each other intensely, you see.'

The men all looked at Anna as if to judge what Henderson could find to dislike so strongly.

'I'm sorry to rush you but we really need to get going. Where is your husband now?' said the older man.

'I don't know. He ran off out of the back door when he heard you coming.'

The young man shook his head. 'If you knew how many nutters go out on those mountains to risk their lives and others for some crazy stunt or challenge… And this one has put his fucking kiddy at risk.'

The older man put his hand on the young man's arm as if to steady him. 'Can I have a description of the child, please?' he asked Nancy.

'Slight build. Brown hair which kinda sticks up all over the place. A tooth missing at the bottom front.'

'Do you know what he was wearing?'

'No. I can't be sure. I didn't see him this morning. He usually wears a pair of blue navy shorts with a T-shirt in this weather. I don't know which one. I'm sorry.'

'How much does he weigh?'

'About 50 pounds'

'And his name is…'

'His name is Henry Ulysses Henderson.'

The man spoke into his walkie-talkie, repeating everything they had said.

'We are going to have to call out further back up to look for the boy and the father if they are now separated, though you do understand that the minor is our first priority?'

Both Nancy and Anna nodded their heads.

All the men left except the older one, who hung back.

'I'm sorry about Trevor. He's a bit of a loose cannon but he knows these mountains better than anyone. His father used to have a sheep farm on one of the highest points. Almost impossible to farm in such a bleak spot. Anyway… just to reassure you… he's the best and we do find lots of people safe and unharmed. The majority, in fact. I'm sure we'll find your boy but we need to get going as soon as we can, see.'

Nancy told him that she thought Henry had been out for at least the last couple of hours.

'Well, it looks like we should start looking around Llandeilo. That's the nearest mountain. That would make sense.' He spoke again into the walkie-talkie attached to his chest, before turning back to the women. 'I'm sure you don't need telling but please leave the search to us. The last thing we need is another lost party. OK? Just give me your landline and mobile numbers. We'll phone you as soon as we've found the boy or if we need any more details but there is no signal in the mountains so you are going to have to sit tight and be patient. The police should be coming along soon. They are always that much slower than us.'

'Good luck,' Anna said as she showed him out of the door.

'I don't know about you,' Nancy said once he'd left, 'but I'm not waiting around here while my son is lost somewhere on those mountains. We've told the rescue team all we know. I have to try to find Henry.'

CHAPTER 24

The two women ran through the house, looking for outdoor clothes. Anna went through the Goldblatts' store of country clothes in the bedroom and found two fleeces and two pairs of socks. Then she looked under the bed to see if there was more stuff stored there. She found a sand-coloured canvas bag and pulled it out. In it was a man's jumper. Her eye was caught by a single screwed-up piece of paper in the waste-paper basket. She picked it out, saw writing on one side and flattened it out with her hand on top of the chest of drawers. It looked like a treasure map. There were simple lines linking an ink drawing of a tree, what looked like a waterfall, a swing, a standing stone, a river and a small house. The house was marked as the start of the trail. She ran downstairs.

'Look, Nancy! Do you think this map might be a version of one your husband might have given to Henry?'

The two women placed an Ordnance Survey map and the hand-drawn map next to each other on the kitchen table.

'I think we should try and contact the rescue team again. Tell them what the map says.'

Anna dialled the number they had been given but it went to voicemail.

'Text him the details. Tell him to find a waterfall,' Nancy said.

Anna put her index finger on the Ordnance Survey map. 'I think we might be able to get there on this little road. Seems to me that it is straight up past Langston Castle.'

'Fine. Come on. Let's go.'

Anna didn't close the door properly in case they needed to get in again. It took five minutes to reach the castle. She parked the car on a verge and they ran through the castle gates and past the National Trust board, then through the keep and over a stile at the back of the castle grounds.

The hill rose steeply behind the small village. The morning's mist hung over the grass so that what lay beyond was obscured, but it looked more like a mountain peak than a hill. The sun was already fighting its way through; catching the dew and making everything sparkle.

'I think that your husband wanted Henry to make his way back around the hill, via the waterfall. If I remember correctly, it's a pretty big hill. I think it's called "Little Black", but it's not so little. The "little" may be a local joke. It'll take us a while,' Anna said.

But Nancy was already running ahead, up the first ascent. Anna found herself struggling to keep up. The terrain became rougher – a mix of dry orange bracken and summer grasses. Soon they were climbing over small boulders and rocks. By the time they got to the top of the hill, the day had cleared and they were able to look out over the sweeping landscape beyond. The hill ran down into a deep valley, beyond which the Black Mountains rose. Anna scanned the line of the ridge. Nancy looked at the maps again and carried on, not stopping, as Anna had hoped, to sit down on one of the flat, warm stones to catch her breath. She took off the fleece, tied it round her hips and followed Nancy.

'According to the map, I think it should be down this way. I think this is the Julip Ridge, but if I know Horace, the final destination will be hidden somewhere. That's what the mountain rescue team won't be able to understand. They won't understand how Horace's mind works, Anna.'

Nancy stood on the flat ridge and held her face up to the air as if sniffing out Henry's scent. Then she shouted out that she could see something and started to run. Anna ran after her. Nancy jumped into a dip in the landscape and then she was on her knees next to a rough wooden structure. She opened the top of it. There were loose straps that looked like they had been hastily hacked. Anna knelt beside it too. The cage was very like the one on the heath made out of closely-woven sticks. The one she had sat in with Henry.

'It's the same as the one on the heath.'

Nancy nodded, her face tight.

Anna touched the leather straps and felt how they curved into the casket. She thought of how Henry must have had to cut his way out.

'Nancy, I think your husband secured the top closed with these leather straps to stop Henry getting out and following him.'

She saw how Nancy's face quivered with pain. She was feeling inside with her hands and pulled out a piece of clementine peel and an apple core, which she held in her pink palm. Both women stared.

'Come on. Where to next? Let's go,' Anna said.

'The waterfall. The waterfall is down in this valley, according to the maps.'

'Why wouldn't Henry just go back over the hill and home?'

Nancy looked at her. 'Because he's seven years old, it is dark and he doesn't know where he is. He's been told that this is the route he has to take and so that is what he will do.'

'OK.'

'I remember that whenever I walked with Horace back home in Ipswich he always said not to take the obvious route. "Don't spoil it by taking the path that hikers take," he would say. "It's no good taking the beaten track. Imagine you are an animal and go cross-country as the crow flies."'

'So that is why Horace's map is just a straight line?'

'Yup. Animals always take the quickest route. They don't bother about who owns the land or which path would be easier or more scenic, do they? The map seems to be pointing towards the river.' She stood up and was off again, marching down the hill, pushing through the thick bracken with her long legs.

It only took ten minutes to get to the bottom, jumping over rocks and scrambling to reach a bridge that crossed the river. Both women lowered themselves down to the grey slippery slate of the riverbank. The river was not high, as it must be in winter, judging by the wood and debris left on the riverbank. Nancy pushed forward and when the bank got too slim, moved into the water and gracefully stepped from stone to stone. Anna had to push herself to keep up. They heard the thudding, joyous spilling sound of water and quickened their pace until they reached the corner. The women found themselves looking down into a deep, thundering pool more than twenty feet below.

'How do we get down?' Anna had to shout to make herself heard.

Nancy looked around and pointed urgently upwards. Anna turned and saw a new blue nylon rope tied tightly to a thick branch. She saw with alarm that the rope fell to the ground right at the side of the waterfall. Both women went closer to the edge, squatting down before looking over. Anna could see that the rock had natural ridges and footholds either side of the ferocious stream.

'My God, Henry must have lowered himself with the rope. I can't see how else he could get down.'

Anna watched numbly as Nancy started to lower herself on to the first ledge, clinging to the rope. Her long body slipped from one ledge to the next until she was well below, looking up at Anna.

Anna forced herself to follow, holding the rope with both hands. When she looked up, she saw the rope slip and jump along the branch. She wondered if the thinner end would snap under her weight, which was considerably more than Nancy's. She felt the sweat prickle on her back as she lowered herself down and felt for the first slim ledge with one foot. She reckoned she had about four more ledges to go; the muscles in her arms and legs shook with fear and strain. With every movement she made, she was aware that Henry had been made to do this, probably alone and with less light. If he could manage it then she could. She looked down. Nancy was calling to her. Encouraging her. Telling her where to put her feet, to hold the rope with one hand, to reach out for a nearby rock, until at last she was down, hands burning from the rope, dripping with her own fear. Both women were breathing heavily.

There was only one path and it led behind the waterfall. Moving sideways, with their faces turned towards the water and their backs to the rock, they moved along it, inch by inch, until they found themselves inside a cave. The noise of the waterfall was terrifying as it echoed round the walls. Inside was a small stone seat carved into the rock, green with moss. It was Anna who saw the tiny scrap of orange peel on it. 'Look, Nancy. Fresh orange peel. It's Henry, isn't it? Henry has sat here recently and eaten another clementine. Don't you think? It has to be.'

'Oh, Anna. I think you're right. He has been here, hasn't he? We're getting closer. Look! The map shows a fallen tree next. There is a drawing of a fallen tree. It seems to be on another small hill.'

Nancy and Anna started to climb up the other side, beyond the waterfall. Nancy seemed filled with a new raw energy, the orange peel giving her hope that perhaps Henry was still alive. Anna followed her until they came out of the wooded area and once again were able to look over the land.

'There's the fallen tree. Come on.' Then Nancy stopped in her tracks and grabbed Anna's arm. Her eyes remained on a spot down below.

'Look, Anna. My God, look. Is it…?'

'Where?'

Anna stared in the direction that so transfixed Nancy. There, far below, in the orange glow of the wiry bracken, illuminated by the bright sunlight, was the tiny, solitary figure of a small child pushing slowly through the undergrowth, walking away from them.

Henry! Henry! It was Henry!

Screaming the child's name at the tops of their voices, the two women raced down over rocks and grasses, not caring that they tripped and scraped themselves as they hurtled downhill. It seemed to Anna as if they were flying to Henry with arms outstretched, their desire to get to him no longer earth-bound. They were soaring through the new morning with the sun behind them, crying out his name. They were hurling themselves down the hillside, rolling down and down, the sound of their voices merging with the snap and rustle of breaking undergrowth, until in a glorious moment he heard them and stopped and turned round. Anna waved her red fleece in the air and screamed his name. Nancy just carried on running towards him. His little face was turned to them, and then Anna and Nancy were neck and neck, racing to get to him through the undergrowth. He watched them without any expression, just blinking his Henry blink, mumbling his brave Henry sound.

When they finally reached him, Anna saw that his hair was plastered to his hot forehead and that he was dressed in camouflage army fatigues. And he was wearing no shoes. Her instinct was to run to him and take his skinny, pale body in her arms and to tell him that everything was all right. Instead, it took all her willpower to hang back and let Nancy be the first to reach him and put her arms around him. To tell him that he was safe.

Nancy wept tears of relief. Anna found herself crying too.

Henry lifted his head and looked at Anna over Nancy's shoulder.

'I'm very tired. Can I have a piggyback, please?'

As Henry moved out of Nancy's grasp, Anna bent to pick him up, but the expression on Nancy's face stopped her.

'You ready, Nancy? OK, turn round. Hold on to me, Henry. I'm going to put you on your mum's back. I expect she's very good at piggybacks, too.'

CHAPTER 25

Nancy and Anna looked up at the hill they had to climb. Nancy stopped stock still. High above them, on the crest of the hill, looking like a great angry giant with his hands on his hips, his grey hair streaming down his shoulders, was Henderson.

Nancy cried out to her husband and for a moment he seemed to look at them. Then he started to run very fast, leaping over bracken and rocks to get to them, his legs longer than ever. Anna screamed for Nancy to run in the other direction and Henry woke up and started to cry. He would take Henry back. They couldn't let him. This couldn't happen. Anna thought for a moment that Nancy was going to take Henry towards her husband, but to her relief she turned and ran with Henry on her back, across the valley in the opposite direction. Anna ran alongside. Henderson was close behind. Anna knew that he would easily catch up with them; she could almost feel his long fingers touching her back.

It was then that they heard the distinct chopping of air. All four looked up to see a helicopter emerging over the hill and swooping in to hover above them. Anna could see the young mountain rescue man leaning out with a megaphone, shouting over the sound of the blades as they cut through the sky.

'Stay where you are. We are going to land on the flattest point. Wait until we have landed before you approach us. I repeat: wait until we have landed before you approach us.'

Nancy was standing stock still with Henry crying in her arms when Anna felt someone grabbing her hair. Henderson. He dragged her backwards through the bracken and threw her down behind a rock, his hand covering her mouth. She could feel his breath on the back of her head. Anna was able to see the men in orange descending from the helicopter carrying a sheet of silver fabric that billowed out and looked for a moment as if it might be pulled into the chaos of wind above them. Anna knew, even while she was being held down, that this was for Henry. To wrap his cold body and get his temperature up. Nancy turned round to look for her, as did the men. She could only plead silently. Take him away. Please take the boy and his mother away to safety. Then they were up and away. Good. Thank God. Henry and Nancy were airborne. The roar of the blades sliced the air and hurt her ear drums.

Only then did she think of herself. She knew why Henderson had seized her rather than Nancy or Henry. She had been the key player. She was part of his game. Had been part of it since the day she met Henry and took him home. Henderson didn't need to hold on to her so tightly though. Why dig his fingers into her? Obviously she would go with him. Where else could she go? He dragged her upright and pushed her ahead. The stones and rocks and scratching grass didn't even hurt her anymore. She was numb to physical pain. She was being frogmarched by an angry maniac. As he swept her along, pushing her upwards towards the blue light, she could hear his panting, but he wasn't looking at her. Neither of them spoke.

At the top of the hill, Anna glanced down, and it was exactly as he had described it in his blog. A river bed, no doubt full in the winter, but now with only a thin vein of water snaking through the bottom of the valley. He had set it up so carefully. He had found a tree with a branch that hung out across the bed, and using his height had managed to throw a thick blue rope over it.

He pulled her roughly by the arm when she stopped to stare at the swing. Henry would never have been able to reach that rope and swing out on his own. It was absurd. It was terrifying.

'Henry wouldn't have been able to do this! You know that, don't you?' Anna screamed.

Not saying a word, he pushed her forward so that she was standing on the edge. She closed her eyes. She knew what was going to happen and that this was it. She whispered to Jason and Nat that she was sorry that she had done this to them. She told them they should have had a mother for a lot longer. She thought of Alphonse and the sweetness of his kisses. She thought of David and how once she had loved him.

Anna was in the sea, looking up at Natasha swimming gracefully above her. The light filtered through the water and lit the beautiful form of her daughter. She was looking up at Jason, who was beat-boxing his way through the school anthem.

Then Henderson was coming up behind her, moving fast. She braced herself for the push that would send her over the edge and downwards. But nothing happened. She felt only a rush of air to one side. When she opened her eyes, he was in midair. Leaping feet first, grey hair spread out behind him. He had not grasped the swing. His long body jumping out into nothingness. He was doing what he had wanted to do when he was a child and Uly had dropped into the ravine. Holding her breath, Anna stepped backwards and watched the final moment in still motion. She heard the crack of head on stone. She saw the birds soaring upwards across the morning sky, disturbed by human flight.

Langston Mountain Rescue call out record spring/summer 2011

No.	Date	Location	Brief details
1	24 Apr 11	*Mid Wales*	Search for missing vulnerable person from care home. Found safe and well some distance from home.
2	26 Apr 11	*Black Mountains*	Search and evacuation of male who collapsed during a walk from home. Dead on arrival.
3	30 Apr 11	*Black Mountains*	Walker with lower-leg injuries on Pen Alt Mawr evacuated to air ambulance.
4	1 May 11	*Shropshire*	Search and evacuation of two 12-year-old boys in hill and forest area.
5	15 June 11	*Black Mountains*	Evacuation of paraglider on north side of Blorenge mountain to 4x4 ambulance. Died before arrival at hospital.
6	6 Jul 11	*Black Mountains*	Assisted evacuation, by RAF SAR helicopter, of seven-year-old child with dehydration and a woman aged 33.
7	6 Jul 11	*Black Mountains*	Search for American man in his late fifties and a British woman aged 47. Man in a confused mental state.
8	6 Jul 11	*Black Mountains*	Male body at the bottom of Blorenge canyon identified as missing American. Woman found at Langston Castle, safe and well.